A MYSTERY NOVEL

LADY in PERIL

(Money Musk)

BEN AMES WILLIAMS

COMPLETE AND
UNABRIDGED

Originally published under the title of

MONEY MUSK

ISBN 978-1-64720-185-2

1

INSPECTOR TOPE—Inspector still by courtesy, despite the fact that he had retired from the force a year or two before—was the figure about whom the incidents here to be related did revolve; but Charlie Harquail must figure briefly in the first of them. Charlie was a reporter on the *Journal*, a lean, long young man who through his acquaintance with the Inspector during the latter's years of active service had more than once been able to beat the town on important stories that had to do with crime. But the Inspector retired, and Charlie married Phoebe Mannis, and Phoebe, though she might respect Tope's abilities, would never love him. So Charlie saw less of the old man as time went on.

But he did come one evening to ask the Inspector a favor, and thus obscurely does this tale begin.

Inspector Tope, since his retirement, took his ease. In the summer he fished, wherever fish were biting within a range of two or three hundred miles; but in the winter he stayed snug at home, like a benign, pink-cheeked, hibernating bear.

He dwelt, before his retirement and also afterward, on the second floor of an old office building on Boyleston Street, in a single room which he had modelled to his uses. There was a bed in a niche in the wall, modestly concealed behind a cretonne curtain during the day; and there were comfortable chairs, and a few books, and one long table entirely devoted to newspapers, which Inspector Tope read with a devout attention. In the grate a coal fire was likely to glow with a comforting warmth; and the old man liked to sit before this fire, his round cheeks bright with the reflected flames. He liked to sit there and talk over old days with his friends when they happened in.

Yet the Inspector was on the whole rather lonely there, as old men are apt to be. It was not that he lacked friends. He had an infinite number of them. But most of them were younger men, engrossed in their own concerns. It is important to choose your friends with an eye to the years they have lived. If they are older than yourself, they may die and leave in your life an empty niche not easily to be filled; and if they are younger, your own advancing years may increase the gap between you. This was what had happened to Inspector Tope. His friends were younger than he, and after his retirement, he was not so often able to serve them. So whenever one of them dropped in to see the old man, it was apt to be from a mild sense of duty. Tope had helped so many people in his time; it was difficult to think of him without remembering some favor he once had done you, still unrepaid. So, many people thought of him, and planned to call in on the Inspector—in a day or two. But not so many of them actually carried out their good intent.

Thus sometimes he had no visitors for days on end; but he did not complain. When they came he met them beamingly; and when they did not come, he read his many newspapers, and stared reflectively into the fire.

He was, by the calendar, older year by year; yet Charlie Harquail could discover no particular change in him tonight. The Inspector's eye was as mildly blue; his cheek as round; his hair as snowy. He stood with the same alertness; his head wagged a little from side to side with that curious suggestion that he smelled some puzzling odor and sought to discover the source; his hands when he walked still swung palms forward as though ready to seize and grip and hold. He had never seemed a formidable figure; Charlie found it hard to remind himself that this old man was formidable now.

Yet though Inspector Tope might be officially retired, his attentive scrutiny of the world was still as keen; his interest in the movements of all those about him was as alert as it had ever been. An old setter dog, too blind and deaf to range the covers with his master, will nevertheless if he chance upon the scent of game come stiffly to a point; and it was so with the Inspector. When that happened which perplexed him, he was instantly curious; it was instinctive with him to begin forthwith by conjecture and inquiry to seek an explanation. And it happened that there was, even before young Charlie tapped at his door this night, such a puzzling matter in the Inspector's mind. He had been intent upon this enigma now for days.

It was about twenty minutes before eight o'clock when Charlie came; and Tope was just back from his solitary dinner. He had returned to his room a quarter of an hour ago; he took off his shoes and put on his slippers and an old dressing gown he liked to wear, and began to read the evening papers, neglecting not a page nor a line. And then Charlie knocked, and the Inspector went to open to him, and recognized the young man with a quick pleasure, and bade him in.

"Glad to see you, son," he said. "It's been quite a while!"

There was no suggestion of reproach in his tones; yet Charlie did feel in some degree disquieted. He gripped the old man's hand, and said he had been very busy, and Tope nodded his understanding and bade the boy sit down. He offered tobacco and a pipe, but Charlie lighted a cigarette instead; and the conversation was for a moment brisk enough, then lagged and died. So the Inspector smiled, and he asked:

"Well, son, what can I do for you?"

Charlie grinned in a shamefaced way. "I suppose you figure I wouldn't have come unless I wanted something," he assented. He added disingenuously: "But as a matter of fact, I've got a couple of tickets to the theatre. Thought you might like to go along."

Tope's eyes were shrewd. "That will be the Booth?" he suggested; and Charlie looked at him astonished. The Inspector chuckled, quite without resentment. "You want to get an interview on what an old policeman thinks of this gangster play? That's the idea, isn't it, Charlie?"

Young Harquail shook his rueful head assentingly. "You always were too numerous for me," he confessed. "But—yes. This show is the hit of the year, you know," he pointed out. "They pull off a wholesale massacre, with machine guns, in the second act. Fire four or five hundred rounds of ammunition right on the stage. Makes more noise than you ever heard in a theatre before. . . ."

Tope shook his head. "You're taking in too much territory, son," he protested. "I remember a show came to town here a good many years ago, and I went to see it. They called it *The Round Up*, and there was a man named Arbuckle played the Sheriff. In the first act he pulled a gun, and an old lady behind me said: 'Mercy, I hope there's no shooting in this!' But in the second act they had an attack by Indians, and a rescue by cavalry, with a rapid-fire cannon and all the rifles in the world going, right on the stage. I guess that could match you for noise!"

Charlie chuckled. "If a thing hasn't happened for ten years, it never happened before," he said. "That's newspaper gospel, Inspector. What do you say? If we're going, we ought to get under way."

Tope considered again; and he said then: "I'll tell you, Charlie. There won't be anyone at your office after the show, will there?"

"Two or three, maybe."

"We'll go down there afterward," the Inspector proposed. "While you're writing your story, you let me look around in your Morgue. There's a man I want to check up on; and you must have some clippings on him."

"I'll look him up for you," Charlie offered; but Tope shook his head.

"No, you turn me loose and leave me alone. This is private. I don't want you to know. Is that a bargain?"

"Why, it's against the rules," Charlie confessed. "But—sure. But what are you up to, Inspector? I thought you'd retired."

"It's just habit with me," Tope admitted. "If I see a thing I don't understand, I'm bound to start poking into it. That's all." He was leaning forward to tie his shoes, panting over the laces; he found his coat and overcoat. "Ready, son," he said presently.

And they went together down the stairs.

The Booth Theatre, where *Typewriters* was in the midst of its record-breaking run, is near the exact middle of the theatrical district. It is semi-isolated from the neighboring buildings, with an alley behind, and another on one side which runs through the block, and on the other side a passage about six feet wide and fifty feet long, which gives access to the stage door. The theatre itself is modern, not over-large. Tope and Charlie tonight found it crowded to the doors; there were standees behind the orchestra. But their own seats were in the fourth row, the side aisle; and they were on the right-hand side of the house.

And while they waited for the curtain, Charlie explained to the Inspector the general scheme of the play. But Tope seemed only mildly interested; he said when Charlie paused:

"I've heard some talk about the leading woman in this show, Charlie!"

"Lola Cyr," Charlie agreed. "You bet! She'll get you! She gets them all. All the men. There's something funny about her, hard to analyze. She's beautiful as the devil, and a swell figure. She wears a sort of turban all the time, a close-fitting hat that covers all her head except her face. You never see her hair, and they say she's as bald as an egg. A man told me—" He hesitated, grinned. "Never mind who," he said. "But this fellow told me he saw her one night without a hat; and he said this cold, hard, flaming beauty of hers, under that ivory bald head, was the most incredibly provocative thing he ever saw. He's not susceptible, either!"

He added: "And Mat Hews is making a hit, too! He never had a part before. They got him right out of some dramatic school in Pasadena, and he comes near stealing the show. He's got a big future, they all say. Then of course Walter Hammond is the star; and there's a cute kid named Kay Ransom . . ."

Tope said thoughtfully: "I remember Hammond. I saw him once, years ago; but I hadn't heard of him for a long time."

Charlie nodded. "He got in a jam about ten years back," he explained. "Some woman died after a supper party; and he was at the party, and the police held him for a while. They didn't pin anything on him; but he couldn't get a job at all for years after that. Then he got a crack at this, and the part fits him like a glove. He's great! He can name his own figure, now!"

And he added: "Matter of fact, everybody connected with this show will be sitting pretty for a while. There she goes. . . ."

And he settled back expectantly as the curtain rose, to sit engrossed in the action that ensued.

But though the play thus laid its spell on Charlie—who had seen it many times before—Inspector Tope was not equally moved. Its fable was conventional. Rival gangs and rival chieftains; a seductress who for love of one betrayed the other; the developing design, the famous massacre in the second act, the unfolding doom which in the end descended on them all. And the whole dark pattern was laid for contrast against the light and tender background of romance; the love of a boy for a girl. . . . Young Mat Hews and Kay Ransom were these two.

Yet for the Inspector, the whole performance lacked reality. The criminals who trod the stage were not true to his experience. He had found such folk on the whole to be a wily, furtive breed, rather than the bold and ruthlessly intelligent figures who were here portrayed. And the murders in the second act seemed to him more suitable to a charnel house than to the theatre.

He was more interested in the individuals who here played their parts. Hammond, he thought, might have been in fact just such a man as he pretended on the stage to be, if he had courage to match his desires. Lola Cyr seemed wholly bold and dark and evil; yet Tope could find her seductive too, and it seemed to him possible that she was in private life a simple, rather friendly soul. Even a lonely one! Also the Inspector liked Mat Hews; and Kay Ransom was pretty and fresh and young.

On the way downtown with Charlie afterward, he told the reporter that while this drama might be theatre, it was not life at all.

"It's hard to put in words," he said. "But—there was make-believe murder on the stage, and yet it wouldn't fool anyone that ever saw the real thing. Murder hits people, son! You can see it in their faces, hear it in their voices. Murder has a smell to it, you might say!"

"The show got hold of me a lot more the second time I saw it," Charlie suggested.

Tope said good-humoredly: "Not likely I'll see it again." The old man was rather proud of his ability to foresee events, but he had just now no remotest anticipation that he would sit once more in this theatre, and watch this same play, and smell murder plain!

He was concerned instead for Charlie's sake. He added apologetically: "But I guess that's not the line of talk you want for your interview!"

Charlie insisted that it was exactly what he wanted; and when they came to the *Journal* office, he showed Tope the reference department and left the old man to his own devices there, while he himself went about the writing of the story he had planned.

The reference department in the office of a great newspaper is a vast repository of information, much of it doomed to a perpetual uselessness. Every day, all available papers are read with scrupulous care; and out of them is cut every story involving the names of persons who are potentially news material. These cuttings are filed away, properly indexed and cross-indexed. So if your name has ever been in the papers, and you happen to be arrested for murder by and by, it will be possible to resurrect all the published reports of your previous escapades and parade them for the enlightenment of a reading public suddenly interested in your least affairs.

The shelves in the *Journal's* reference department were thickly filled with envelopes, each marked with a name; and Inspector Tope sought for one marked with the name of Clarence Peace. He found it and was surprised to see how well filled it was. For half an hour he scanned the clippings it contained, with an attentive care; and before Harquail was done, the Inspector was infinitely wiser than he had been before.

Then Charlie finished, and wished him to read and to approve the interview, and Tope did so, and Charlie went to drop the typed sheets in the editor's box.

He came back with questions. "Find what you want in there?" he asked; and Tope nodded cheerfully.

"Plenty," he assented. "I didn't look to find so much as I did."

Charlie grinned at him. "See here," he urged. "What's it

all about? Battle, murder, arson, theft, fraud? Give me a line, Inspector. Is there a story in it anywhere?"

Tope hesitated. "Why, not yet, son," he decided. "There may be, later though. When a man starts out along a road, you can't be quite sure where he'll end." He said almost sorrowfully: "Maybe I've made a business of murder too long; but it seems to me sometimes that almost any crooked trick can turn into a murder before it's done."

Harquail protested: "Say, you're making it tough for me! I don't talk much, Inspector. Let me in on it. Let me watch the show, so I can be ready when it breaks."

But Tope shook his head. "If there's a story here, you'll never get it from me," he declared. "It's not mine to give you." He added: "But as a matter of fact, there isn't any story, far as I know!"

"Then what are you after?" Charlie urged; and Tope said with a chuckle:

"Why, I'm just trying to find out why a friend of mine hasn't been around to see me lately, son."

Harquail colored with a quick embarrassment. "Are you riding me?" he asked. "Well, I haven't any comeback. Whoever it is, he'll probably come around when he wants something, the same way I did. I guess that's the answer, Inspector?"

Tope chuckled. "Don't worry, Charlie," he told the younger man. "I'm glad to see you any time." And he added then, almost as though he wished to reassure the other: "If there's a story in this, Dave Howell can give it to you."

"What will I ask him?" Harquail urged.

Tope's eyes were twinkling: "Why, you tell him I was wondering why he hasn't been around."

So a moment later he said good night to the young man, and set out for home; and except for a brief appearance on the night of the first murder, Charlie does not enter into this chronicle again.

2

THIS Dave Howell of whom Tope spoke was a police inspector whose particular province was frauds and defalcations; and while he was a much younger man than Inspector Tope, they had long been friends. After Tope's retirement, Dave had been a regular visitor till within two months or so. Then he ceased to come, and Tope began to wonder why, and to seek an answer to his own question.

After his word to Charlie Harquail, he expected Howell to come; so he was not surprised when the next morning Dave knocked on his door. Tope opened to him smilingly, and made Dave comfortable, with a jar of tobacco at his elbow, matches at his hand. Dave lighted his pipe, and Tope spoke casually of this and that, and he watched the other wisely.

Inspector Howell was a big, heavy-shouldered man, with lumbering wits, but with a tenacity about him that was apt to bring him results in the end. Usually he was physically calm as big men are apt to be; but today his hand moved aimlessly about the table beside his chair, picking up small objects and setting them down again; he struck many matches and held them to the bowl of his pipe, even though it was already burning freely; and he was so abstracted that he made only the briefest replies to Tope's remarks, until the Inspector asked at last good-humoredly:

"Well, Dave, this Peace got you worried, has he?"

And at that Dave's abstraction instantly did vanish. He fixed on the older man a level stare of deep surprise; and he demanded in an incredulous tone:

"What makes you ask that? What do you know about Peace?"

"Not much," Tope assured him, but there was a twinkle of amusement in his mild blue eyes. "Not much! Only what I read in the papers. I know he's a lawyer, and a bachelor and a sportsman. Used to be a crack polo player, rode to the hounds and all that. And I know he had charge of the Jervis Trust; and I know he was hurt in an auto smash about two years ago; and I know he was dropped from the Unity Club last winter, and why. And I know he lived in an apartment on the Avenue. And I know he hasn't been there the last two months or so."

Dave grinned. "You didn't read all that in the papers!" he protested.

"I hear things," Tope confessed; and he beamed and wagged his head. "People tell me things, and I hear things, and I read things, and I do a lot of wondering. But you go on and tell me, Dave. What's Peace done—besides go away?"

"Plenty," Howell said morosely. "He's looted the Jervis Trust! And he's skipped! And I was wise to him!" He pounded his knee in a slow fury. "I was wise to him, but I let him get away. That's why I haven't slept much this last two months, old man."

Tope filled his pipe and lighted it. He took it in his plump hands and rubbed the black bowl between his palms; and he said thoughtfully: "Go on and talk, Dave. Do you good to talk about it. Maybe you'll talk yourself into some idea."

And he put the pipe in his mouth, precisely in the middle, so that it seemed to bisect his pleasant round face; and he listened with a deep attention while Howell put the facts as he knew them in order for the older man.

He began at the beginning, with the Jervis Trust. Dana Jervis, when he died, left a considerable estate, the income to be divided equally between his children, Clint and Clara. "They're not around here," Dave explained. "Young Clint's been seeing Paris, the last year or two; and Clara's in California, studying dramatics, and having herself a time." And he went on to say that the estate consisted almost wholly of real property; an office building, a store block on a valuable downtown corner, some rentals in the congested West End, four large apartment houses on the Avenue.

"They have an office in their own building," he said. "There's an old man named Beede, a sort of clerk; and a youngster named Randall, and a woman named Miss Moss. She's fifty if she's a day, and hard as nails. Theoretically, she's Peace's stenographer; but actually she ran the office when he wasn't there."

And most of the time, he added, Peace was not there. He was accustomed to come once or twice a week to consult with Miss Moss and approve her courses and depart again. For the rest; the affairs of the Jervis Trust were in her hands.

"But the Trust didn't suffer," Howell assured Tope. "Miss Moss has a pretty shrewd, level head. All the income was supposed to go to the children; but she managed to increase the principal without cutting down on them. They never complained, because they had all they could spend; and the Trust was getting bigger all the time."

He hesitated, and Tope interposed: "They're not here, you say?"

"No," Dave told him. "The boy, Clint; he's studying art, or architecture or something, in Paris. I guess most of the art he studies is in the nude. He raised the devil in college; and he's kept up the same game ever since. From all I hear, he's one of these quiet ones till he gets started, and then he's a skyrocket with a cannon cracker on its tail. And the girl's as bad! Junior League and all that, but she got restless. Went to California to go into the movies, and couldn't get a job, and went to some dramatic school out there. She got herself into a jam with a man, a while back, got her name in the papers. Maybe you saw it."

Tope made it his business to read every line in the local papers every day, but he did not respond to this suggestion now; and Dave said apologetically:

"I don't know as there's anything really wrong with either of them except too much money; but that's enough to ruin a kid, I suppose. Anyway, that's their rep! But it hasn't anything to do with what I started to say."

Tope suggested: "Except that it was the money they had, and the money Miss Moss made for them, that kept them going."

"Sure," Dave agreed. "And she was making plenty! The Trust was like a snowball, from all I can find out. Getting bigger right along. Up to about two years ago."

"Peace had his accident about that time, didn't he?" Tope

suggested. "I remember he got a bad crack on the head, a fracture, nearly died."

"He got a big gash across the top of his head," Howell assented. "And he lost the toes off his right foot, halfway back to his ankle."

Tope's pipe was hissing cheerfully as Howell went on:

"I guess he was pretty sick, but he got over it. And he got fat, after that, too. Probably because he stopped exercising. Anyway, he put on weight fast."

"And then the Unity Club dropped him," Tope prompted. "Something about a poker game?"

"Last spring," Howell agreed. "And I heard about that, so I began to look him up. The market was booming, and any man with other people's money in his hands might make a mistake, if he had a shady streak in him. So I poked around a little.

"I found out that the Trust was mortgaging its real estate and investing the money in stocks. All blue chip stuff, bought outright; but I wasn't satisfied. I'd rather stop a fire before it starts; but there wasn't anything I could put a finger on."

He hesitated. "I did a fool thing, then," he confessed. "But I wanted to size up the man, so I went to see him. I told him I'd heard that one of the clerks in the office had got away with some money; asked him if he wanted to prosecute. He was friendly and agreeable and all that; but I didn't get anything out of him. Far as I could see, he acted like any other man would have acted."

He was silent for a moment, staring at nothing. "I've gone off half-cocked all through this thing," he admitted. "After I saw him, I got worried for fear he'd skip, so I set Haddon to keep an eye on him. That was maybe ten weeks ago. Haddon tailed him right along. Then about two months ago, Peace bought a ticket on the night train to Washington. He took a taxi from his apartment to the Booth Theatre." He did not see Tope's eyes suddenly become more intent. "He knew this Walter Hammond, playing in that show there, and he went back stage to see Hammond. And he never came out."

Tope asked swiftly: "What happened? What did Hammond say?"

"Said he left Peace in his dressing room when he went on in the second act, and never saw him after that."

Tope nodded, and Dave made a weary gesture.

"Well," he said, "I waited a day or two, and when he didn't show up, I went to the Trust offices to see Miss Moss. I put my cards on the table, asked her to check up on him. The Trust had a vault in the basement of the building. He and Miss Moss had keys and access. She found that most of the securities supposed to be there were gone."

"She hadn't missed anything before?" Tope interjected.

Howell shook his head. "No reason why she should!" he explained. "He attended to that end of things. The securities had been filed away in envelopes, each one marked; and he'd put blank paper in place of them. I figure he converted them into Libertys, stuff we can't trace, good anywhere at all!" His tone was deep in hopeless wrath.

The old man nodded. "Where did Miss Moss think he'd head for?" he asked cheerfully.

"She didn't know!" Howell assured him. "But I've checked every way out; he didn't take a train, and he didn't take a boat, and he hadn't ridden in an automobile since his smash. Tope, he's right here in town. That's my hunch! That's what's getting me!"

The older man seemed to consider for a while, and he inquired at last: "Dave, did his hair cover that scar on his head?"

"The scar didn't show," Howell said readily.

"Did he walk with a limp?"

"Yes. Yes, with a sort of thump when the toe of his shoe came down."

"And he had got fat, after that accident?"

"Yes."

Tope puffed precisely at his pipe; he sat for a long minute like a plump old statue, beaming at the fire, while Howell stirred in a restless impatience. Then Tope asked:

"Miss Moss a good business woman, you think?"

"She's smart as they come," Howell agreed. And he added: "I've seen her two-three times since Peace ducked. She's running the whole show, now, of course; and she's different! As if she liked it."

"The estate hurt bad?" Tope asked.

"Around four hundred thousand," Howell declared. And his fist knotted on his knee. "Four hundred thousand in Libertys, floating around somewhere, Tope! That's what I'm shooting at; what I've got to find."

Tope cleared his throat; he puffed his pipe, he fell into a protracted silence, sitting motionless, his eyes half-closed, staring at the fire. Now and then he wagged his head as though brushing some thought aside; now and then he nodded as though accepting some conclusion fixed and sure. And Howell waited patiently enough, till at last the old man stirred. He rose, and he said briskly:

"Dave, let's go call on Miss Moss. I'd like to see her, talk to her. She might have some idea!"

Howell stared at him, surprised at something in the other's tone. "She doesn't know a thing," he protested. "I'll bet on that! She's straight as they come!"

"Maybe!" Tope assented. "But just the same, I'd like to talk to her. Even if she wasn't in on this, she might know something you didn't think to ask. Let's go see."

"Blast it!" Howell insisted. "It's Peace I want, and the four hundred thousand! You won't find him in the Jervis Trust offices."

"Have you looked there?" Tope asked, with a quizzical grin; and Howell uttered an explosive negative. "Then you'd better!" said Tope. "Because you haven't found him, so one of the places where you haven't looked is where he's bound to be."

Howell stared at him. He asked incredulously: "You think Miss Moss is in it?"

And Tope said: "Why, it looks to me that a real good business woman ought to notice if a man got away with four hundred thousand in bonds, right under her nose!"

Howell shook his head. "You're wrong!" he declared. "I'll bet on her. You'll see."

"See her; yes! That's what I want to do, Dave," Tope mildly insisted. "Let's go along. . . ."

The offices of the Jervis Trust had about them that almost pretentious shabbiness which austere respectability so often likes to wear. On the second floor of an ancient building on

Tremont Row, their windows looked out into an alley, and sunlight seldom entered there. When Dave Howell and Inspector Tope opened the door and stepped inside, the place was all in shadow; dusk filled the corners of the one big room.

Tope, with a quick glance, saw desks and filing cabinets and record cases round the walls; and an old man on a high stool at the ledger desk by the further window must be Beede. Then a younger man approached to greet them, and Inspector Howell asked: "Where's Miss Moss?"

"At lunch," the other returned. "But she'll be here within ten minutes."

"Where's Randall?" Howell inquired. "What's become of him? Is he gone?"

"I've taken his place here," the young man replied, and he had a smile which Tope approved. He continued: "If you'll wait, Miss Moss will be here presently. Or perhaps I . . ."

But before he could finish, the door beside them opened; and he broke off, added quickly: "Here she is now. Miss Moss, these gentlemen . . ."

Tope had been watching this young man, but he swung now to the woman, and with a quick surprise. Dave had said she was hard as nails; but Tope had an instant impression that Dave might be wrong in his appraisal. She had been when she came in almost radiant; but in this first moment when she confronted them, Tope saw a pulse stir in her throat and quiet there.

Then she spoke to Dave Howell; and Inspector Howell introduced the older man.

"Inspector Tope is an old friend of mine," he explained. "I've been asking some advice from him about tracing Mr. Peace. He wanted to talk to you."

Miss Moss nodded. "Certainly," she agreed, and she led them toward her desk. These three sat down together there. The window was at her back as she faced them, so that her countenance was shadowed as she waited for what they might have to say.

Dave left the matter in the hands of the older man; but he was astonished at the turn the immediate conversation took. For Tope looked around the long, dusky room; and he said at last as though in idle curiosity:

"Looks like you people still had enough to keep you busy!"

"We must build something out of nothing," Miss Moss agreed. "That's our task now."

"As bad as that?" Tope protested; and she hesitated, said then:

"Quite! There isn't much left of the Trust except the realty, and that is heavily mortgaged. The interest charges, and taxes, and repairs will eat up most of the rentals. Of course, with strict economy, the estate can be brought back, in time."

Tope nodded. His eyes were mild, yet they watched her keenly. He said at last:

"I had two or three questions I wanted to ask you, Miss Moss, in case you could answer them. You knew Mr. Peace better than most, I expect."

"I expect," she assented.

"Worked for him long?"

"I was Mr. Jervis' secretary," she explained, "before he died. For fifteen years. And he asked me to stay on with Mr. Peace here."

Tope seemed to weigh this information thoughtfully. "Mrs. Jervis died a good while ago, didn't she?" he asked.

"When Clara was born," Miss Moss assented, in a low tone.

The old man nodded, as though abandoning this matter. "Now about Mr. Peace," he suggested. "What did he look like? Scar on his head didn't show, Inspector Howell tells me."

"No," she said. "He brushed his hair over it. He wore his hair short, before; but after he was hurt, Mr. Peace went away for a rest and vacation, and let his hair grow longer, and when he came back, he brushed it across, parted it on the side."

"And he limped?" Tope suggested.

"There was a little halt in his gait," she assented.

"He wear a mustache?"

"Not since the accident. He did before!"

"And he'd put on weight?"

"Yes," she agreed. "He wasn't a tall man, but he grew almost stout. He gave up his polo, sold his horses after the accident, you know."

"Take a man that's been used to exercise and stops all of a sudden, he's apt to put on weight," Tope agreed. "Hair was black, wasn't it?"

"Yes."

"How old a man?"

"Near fifty," she replied. "But he never seemed so old till these last two years."

He nodded, as though she pleased him. Then he rested his hands on his chubby knees, leaning a little forward. "It's funny," he suggested, "that a man his age hadn't begun to get gray. With black hair, they usually do."

She smiled faintly. "I thought at one time he was beginning to," she confessed. "Some years ago."

Tope chuckled. "Well, you can't always count on it," he agreed. "With a bachelor, specially." He leaned forward again. "Now take it just before he went away. You see much of him, the last week or two?"

"He wasn't in the office for a week before," she assured him. "Till the day he disappeared."

"Came in that day, did he?"

"Yes."

"What for?"

She hesitated. "Why—routine business," she explained, something almost evasive in her tone.

"What kind of business?" he insisted. "Anything about the building he lived in, Miss Moss?"

She looked at him acutely. "Why do you ask that?" she countered; but before he could reply, she went on: "Because as a matter of fact, that was the case."

"You don't say!" he protested. "Why, I was just shooting in the dark!"

Howell paid attention; for Inspector Tope was not one to shoot in the dark. There was always some purpose behind his questions. But Miss Moss seemed to find nothing incredible in this explanation.

"The superintendent of the building up there had resigned a few days before," she explained. "I had hired a new man, Michelsen. Mr. Peace didn't know this till I told him. Details of that sort I usually handled alone."

Tope seemed faintly puzzled. "Then if Peace didn't know that, what did he come in about?" he asked.

She hesitated. "Oh, he came to sign the payroll," she said at last.

"Nothing else?" Tope insisted. "Anything about repairs up there, or the help?"

She was silent for a long moment; asked then: "Is that another—shot in the dark?"

"Why, no," Tope explained. "A new superintendent might want to change the help."

She seemed to consider, shook her head. "No," she said. "It wasn't Michelsen's doing. But Mr. Peace told me he had discharged the janitor that day; caught the man stealing his neckties. I had wanted to let him go before, but Mr. Peace had always defended him."

Tope nodded. "So Michelsen had to hire a new janitor?" he suggested.

"Yes," she agreed; and Tope asked her casually:

"You see this new man?"

She might have been trying to remember; and she said at length, reluctantly: "Why, yes. His name is Burke. He heard about the vacancy, came to me about it. I sent him to Michelsen, and Michelsen took him on."

"How long was this after Peace fired the other one?"

"That same day. Late that afternoon."

"The day Peace disappeared?" he asked, and she assented.

Tope seemed to sigh. "Well, we're not getting anywhere," he decided. "Inspector Howell here, he's got an idea that Mr. Peace is still in town, playing hide and seek with us."

"I don't think so," she objected.

"I don't know," Tope argued. "It looks like if a man five feet six, and weighing close on to a hundred and sixty, and walking with a limp, had gone anywhere, someone would have seen him go."

Miss Moss made no comment on this; and Tope sat silent for a moment, looking at his hands where they rested on his knees. He remarked as though to himself: "I suppose you didn't have anything to do with handling the stocks and so on."

She shook her head: "No. The real estate was my particular province."

So Tope rose a little wearily; and he picked up his hat from her desk and turned it in his hands. "Well, thank you, ma'am," he said. He hesitated, faced her again. "What did you say was the name of the superintendent up there?" he asked.

"Michelsen," she repeated.

"Know him by sight, do you?"

"Certainly. He comes in here once a month to get the payroll for the building."

Tope wiped his mouth with his hand: "So the janitor, and the rest of them, they don't have to come in."

"Oh, no!" she assured him.

"But you hired this Burke? This janitor?"

She hesitated. "Why—yes, in a way," she confessed at last in a still tone.

Tope nodded, and he thanked her again. "Well, Dave, I guess we might as well go along," he decided; and Inspector Howell rose. There was in his bearing disappointment, but no surprise at their failure here. The two men moved together toward the door.

But at the door Tope stopped and turned to look back at Miss Moss with a deep attention. She had not moved; she still sat at her desk, watching them. Her countenance was in shadow so that he could not see the expression in her eyes.

Yet he was an observant man. There was something in the very set of her head and the posture of her shoulders as she sat there silhouetted against the light which seemed to him eloquent. He had an impression that she was like a runner, waiting for the gun.

And there was fear in her. He wished, absurdly, to go back and somehow comfort the woman sitting so alertly there.

3

WHEN they left the offices of the Jervis Trust, the old man and Inspector Howell took a taxicab; and Howell gave the driver the address of Tope's lodgings on Boylston Street. On the way, Dave asked a question or two; but Tope did not answer him. The Inspector sat silent, frowning as though in some deep perplexity; and when they came to their destination, his silence still persisted.

They alighted, and Howell paid the driver, and they went up the single flight of stairs in silence and Tope unlocked his door.

Within the room, Tope sat down in his great chair again, and Howell asked: "Well, did you get anything?"

But Tope made a sound which was neither assent nor negation; and Howell contented himself with waiting for a while. He crossed to the windows and stood looking down into the street; and Tope sat still, his lips moving faintly, nodding now and then as though he tallied off certain considerations in his mind.

By and by Howell turned to watch him. The old man was like a bland Buddha there, only his head moving now and then; and Howell's nerves were raw from the long strain of failure. Irritation grew in him; Tope seemed so nearly asleep. Howell rated his own folly in supposing for a moment that he might find any help or hint of counsel here. He moved at last in a sore impatience, crossed the room and laid his hand upon the door.

Then Tope did speak. He seemed to rouse; and he asked mildly: "Where you going, Dave?"

"Hit the sidewalks," Howell said angrily. "Keep moving. What else is there to do?"

"Why, you might as well go get Peace, I guess," Tope told him, almost regretfully; and Howell stared at him. He gripped the knob on the door as though for support, and there was an eager haste dawning in his eyes.

"Go get him?" he repeated. "Go where?"

"Go where he is," Tope replied, smiling faintly. The old man was still young enough to have an almost childish satisfaction in the miracles he sometimes did perform. "Go where he is, Dave. That's the best place to go, it looks to me!"

"You know where he is?" Howell cried; and Tope said:

"It wouldn't surprise me if I did."

"Then come on!" Howell cried. "Let's go!"

But Tope sat still. "I don't figure it's any of my business," he remarked, half to himself. "I'm not a policeman any more. Maybe this isn't my business at all." Howell protested in a furious impatience, but Tope shook his head. "I'm not going," he decided. "You can go!"

"Go where?" Howell cried. "Hurry, man!"

"There's no hurry," Tope assured him. "He'll wait. He's been there two months. He won't run away."

Howell came striding toward him, trembling with impatience. "All right," he assented. "What's the answer? Where is he? How do you know?"

Tope hesitated; he sighed at last, and he said almost reluctantly: "Why, Dave, I always did play my hunches hard. This is a hunch, that's all. Maybe I'm wrong. I haven't checked up on it; haven't seen him. But Miss Moss told you where he is. Without meaning to."

"I didn't hear her," Howell insisted. "Where do you think he is? How do you know so much, old man?"

The Inspector chuckled in a dry mirth. "Reminds me of when I was a boy," he remarked. "My father had a horse—we lived in a little town up-State—and one day the horse got out of the pasture and got lost and we couldn't find him. There was an old fellow named Ahab something; and he found the horse and brought him home. Father asked how he did it, and Ahab said: 'Waal, I set and figgered whur I'd have put for if I was a hoss, and I did, and he wuz.' "

But Howell exploded: "What's that got to do with Peace?"

So Tope told him patiently: "Here's the way I see it, Dave. I started wondering how I'd go about it to disappear. And it struck me, by and by, that nobody ever sees much of a janitor. How many times did you ever see one, Dave?

Take it in a big building, no one ever goes down cellar unless the janitor doesn't answer the telephone when you want some steam . . ."

Howell cried: "You mean to say . . ."

"I've a notion," said Tope carefully, "that Peace made up his mind to what he was going to do, two or three years ago. I guess he figured the whole thing. But he had sense; and he knew that if he just grabbed the money and ran, someone would nab him, sure. Some sort of disguise, or impersonation or something is likely to figure in any big fraud or embezzlement, Dave. You know that. So Peace would plan on a disguise. But it's hard to put on a false beard and make it look natural. So Peace might play the game with reverse English. He'd disguise himself first, so that what you thought he looked like wasn't what he really looked like at all. You think Peace was a fat little black-haired man with a limp. Well, my guess is his hair wasn't black. He'd dyed it for years, or he wore a wig. And I guess he didn't have to limp. A man gets used to a foot cut off that way, so he walks natural enough. And he could take the fat off in a month or so, if he wanted to; if there was some place he could hide out while he was doing it. He'd need to be out of sight for a spell, while he was getting thin again."

He hesitated, added then: "So I figure that when he got ready, he fired the janitor and went down cellar and took on his job!"

Howell ejaculated: "Are you just guessing, Tope? You know anything about it at all?"

And Tope said almost irritably: "I'm guessing, if you want it that way. Call it a guess, or a hunch, or anything you want. I know this Burke, this new janitor, has been losing weight ever since he took the job."

"How do you know?"

Tope exclaimed: "Man, I've been nosing around for two weeks now! When you quit showing up here, I asked Hagan one night; and he told me what was on your mind. I never could keep my finger out of a pie, Dave. That's why I sent for you. Why I told Harquail to see you. . . ."

Howell said thoughtfully: "I'll grab him! But what about the money, Tope? Where's he put that? Any idea at all?"

Tope was silent for a long moment; he said at last: "I don't know. I had it all figured out, before I saw Miss Moss. It looked to me she must be in on it. But now I don't know. She's all right, I'd say."

"Sure," Dave agreed in a heedless haste. "I told you that!" He pounded on his knee. "He's been right under my nose, all this time!" he cried, and he gripped Tope's arm. "Man, I hand it to you!" he exclaimed.

Tope nodded indifferently. "All right," he said. "But Dave —who's that young fellow took Randall's place in the Trust office?"

"What difference does that make?" Howell exploded. He swung toward the door. "I'm going along!" he cried. "I'll bring Peace in to see you half an hour from now!" There was a great exultation in the man. He slammed the door behind him; Tope heard his feet pounding down the stairs.

The old man left behind here returned to his thoughts again. This matter had seemed to Dave Howell simple enough, when once Tope made it clear; but Dave was only interested in results. Tope found in it much to perplex him still. There were, or seemed to him to be, many questions that must still be answered. If Miss Moss were as good a business woman as she appeared to be, how was it possible that she had not detected the thefts in time to prevent them? If Peace and Burke, the new janitor, were in fact the same, how could she have failed to recognize Peace in Burke when the latter came to ask her for this job?

Before he saw the woman, Tope had been ready to believe in her complicity; but he was not thus ready now. Something intangible and hard to define had passed between him and Miss Moss while they talked together this afternoon; and the old man was conscious of it, without understanding what it was.

There dwelt in him nowadays so often a deep loneliness; the men he had known were so apt to treat him as one outside their lives; the world in which he had borne a part permitted him that part no more. Yet strangely, when he spoke to Miss Moss, he was not lonely. He had expected from Howell's description to find in her a woman hard and shrewd and calculating; instead she seemed to him quite otherwise.

Wise, yes; and steady, and firm, and brave. Yet curiously tender, too. And he had thought he saw in her something like a sudden fear—not on her own account at all.

He reflected that matters turned so often thus contrariwise. Your advance estimates of a person were so apt to be overturned when you met that person face to face. With a complete inconsequence, Tope decided that the Jervis children, for all their ill repute, might prove to be fine wholesome youngsters if you knew them well. Then his thoughts turned back to Miss Moss again.

His own hard common sense told him insistently that she could not have been wholly blind to Peace's design; yet he was equally sure that to be faithless to her trust was not in her. And for half an hour after Howell left him, he tried to read this riddle. He remembered her every glance and intonation; how when she came in the door her eyes touched the young man who had first greeted them; how that pulse stirred in her throat when she saw them standing there. She must have guessed why they had come. . . . Yet how steady she was, and serene, while he had questioned her. Courage dwelt in her, then, and wisdom; and Tope thought there might also abide in her a valorous audacity, a recklessness of consequence.

But nothing sinister or dark. Of this he was sure. Yet the facts, so far as he could perceive them, were eloquent against her; he could read no other meaning into them. She must have guessed Peace's purpose; she must answer to the accusation of complicity.

The old Inspector, waiting for news from Dave Howell, confessed these things to himself. Nevertheless, he decided, what she had done was not his affair. He was no longer a sworn officer of the law; there was no obligation on him to punish evil doers. If Howell did not perceive that she must be guilty too, Tope would not enlighten him. Not if the money were recovered, Peace laid securely by the heels. . . .

Then the 'phone rang, and Dave was on the wire, full of exasperation, full of baffled rage.

"Tope?" he shouted. "It was him! But he's gone! An hour ago. Quit the job and left. But I'll have him inside twenty-four hours."

Tope stood rigidly attentive. "Gone?" he repeated in a flat tone.

"He lived here," Howell explained. "Had a room in the basement. But he'd been sick, lost a lot of weight. He told Michelsen today that he couldn't stand the work any longer. Quit. Walked out. But I'll get him now. . . ."

And Tope heard the receiver clash down on the hook; and he stayed there, very still, and there was trouble in his eyes.

For Miss Moss, he perceived quite clearly, must have sent the man some word, warned him away. But if that were so, then there was an alliance between these two. . . . She was corrupt, dishonest after all!

It was incredible, outside all human sense and nature! Tope could not accept the thing as it lay; yet there was no escape for him. He crossed the room and sat down heavily in his chair, and he was suddenly tired and old. Until today he had never seen Miss Moss, had never even heard her name. Yet now when she was discovered as a thief—or the partner of a thief—the very world turned black before his eyes!

He fought against belief; and when his own hard sense forced him to believe, he began to grope in his thoughts for some explanation that would plead for her. But it was a long time before he found at last a possibility.

At the thought, he came to his feet; he crossed to the telephone to test this new hypothesis. Yet with his hand upon the instrument he paused. Suppose this explanation he suspected were not true; suppose she were in fact as guilty as she seemed!

He shook his head. No matter what the pain, he could not rest without knowing. He lifted the receiver, and gave the number of the Jervis Trust offices, and he licked his lips with a nervousness strange to see in this man. A masculine voice answered, and Tope began to perspire faintly. He had to swallow hard before he could speak. He asked then:

"Jervis Trust?"

"Yes, sir."

"I'd like to speak to Clint Jervis."

"This is he," said the voice at the other end of the wire. "Who is speaking?"

But the old Inspector gently broke the connection; he put the telephone aside and stood smiling, with a light of contented comprehension in his eyes. He could understand, now. The world was well again.

Yet there was a measure of vanity in the old man; he was not willing that Miss Moss should think he had been befooled! Also, there were other reasons not clear even to himself why he wished to see this woman again. He put on his hat and coat and went downstairs and hailed a taxicab and gave the driver the address of the Jervis Trust office, on Tremont Row.

While the cab picked its way through traffic, the Inspector had a sudden sense that he was embarked upon an expedition whose eventual consequences he could not foresee. But he put the thought aside as lacking all foundation. Not even his keen senses could smell out a murder still a dozen hours away. . . .

There was never any mystery about Inspector Tope's ability to solve the most obscure enigma. He was a simple and straightforward man, who happened to have the trick of perceiving the obvious, and fastening upon it, and refusing to be shaken from his hold. He could, and upon occasion did, display a vast patience, and a bold audacity, and a tireless acceptance of facts as facts, regardless of how ridiculous or incredible they might seem. But this was all. He would himself have told you that there was no particular skill involved in his exploits; that any man might have done the same.

Nevertheless the Inspector had enjoyed his preeminence; for like anyone else, he had his vanity. Also, though he was the mildest man in the world, he could be relentless too. Once the chase was up, he was like a good sight hound which will never yield nor waver. So he had not been used to failure; and this vanishing of Clarence Peace at the very moment of prospective capture might be called failure, and so might have been disquieting. But Tope's interest, even before he sent Howell to apprehend the defaulter, had shifted from Peace to Miss Moss. Tope thought he could judge a man—or a woman; and he had judged her and found her loyal, and devoted to the trust she served. Yet it was certain in his mind that she knew where Peace was hiding; it was certain, when Peace escaped, that she had warned the man in time for him to get away.

And at first this hurt and shocked Tope deeply; till he began to guess her underlying motive. When he now set out to see her again, he told himself that he did so only in order to confirm that conjecture; yet there was more than this. He wished to see Miss Moss again—for whatever reason! Without knowing why, without seeking to define his own desires, he yet wished to see her.

Just now as he rode toward the Trust offices, he recalled her as she had been an hour or so ago; and he understood that she must have been in a trembling terror then. Yet she had held herself so steadily, her front was brave and firm. He knew a strange, protective tenderness toward this woman he had not seen till today; he wished to help her and comfort her and to defend her against the world.

For she might need defending, if Dave Howell learned that it was she who sent word to Peace to make haste away. Dave was a bulldog not easily to be robbed of his prey.

Tope had no proof that she had warned Peace; he had only certainty. Proof is doubtful and can be overthrown; but when a man has a certainty in his own mind, even though he can not prove what he believes, he is nevertheless armored against all contingencies. Tope more than once in his professional career had become certain of the guilt of an individual, had directed his actions as though that certainty were capable of proof. And chance or circumstance had somehow come to fight for him, to make good his cause.

So now he was certain; so now he came back to the Jervis Trust to see Miss Moss again!

When he opened once more the door of the single big room which served the Trust as an office, all here was as it had been before, with old Beede at his stool, and Miss Moss at her desk, and the young man whom Tope had liked a while ago poring through a heap of leases from the files.

Tope stood for a moment in the open doorway, and his glance rested speculatively upon Beede yonder. The man was spare and stooped and gray; he bore the marks of years, years spent at his ledgers here. The Inspector was a surprisingly imaginative man; and it occurred to him that in Beede a fierce loyalty might dwell. Such old men, bound all their lives to one service, are sometimes capable of devoted and audacious actions. Tope wondered what Beede would say—or do—if he should confront some day this Clarence Peace who had looted the Trust which Beede served.

But this was no more than an instantaneous reflection. Then Tope took off his hat and walked across to where Miss Moss sat, with that curiously springy gait which was characteristic of the old man, despite his age. She watched him approach, but she made no sign or movement; and he sat down before her, his hat upon his knees. What light there was from the window behind her fell full upon his face, but hers was shadowed still.

He said directly, and his eyes were twinkling: "Well, ma'am, he got away!"

She watched him without replying; yet he thought her shoulders moved as though the muscles tightened there.

"The janitor up there," he explained. "That man you hired! And fired an hour ago!"

"Oh!" she whispered. She made no pretense that she did not understand. It was as though she perceived that this was a man not readily deceived. But neither did she seek to excuse or justify herself at all.

Tope smoothed his hat thoughtfully. "You know, Miss Moss," he said reassuringly, "I was on the police force a good many years. But I'm retired. I'm not on duty now. I don't have to do a thing, just because the law says so and so. It takes a load off a man sometimes."

She did not speak; and he looked across the room at the young man busy there. Then his glance returned to her. He asked slowly:

"I suppose Clint Jervis and his sister have had to slow down some, since this happened, haven't they?"

And since she did not answer at once, he said in a grave insistence, curiously comforting: "Ma'am, you can talk to me. And I want you to."

When she spoke presently, it was more to herself than to him. She said carefully:

"So far as we can find out, Mr. Peace took about four

hundred thousand dollars' worth of securities. They represented money borrowed on the Jervis real estate at six per cent. That means that Clint and Clara lose about a thousand dollars a month in income; each one of them. Yes, they have had to—slow down." She added, with a faint smile somehow appealing:

"Of course, they still have a hundred or so. That isn't poverty, but it seems like very little to them!"

He asked, with a nod toward the young man yonder: "What's Clint doing here? Checking up on things?"

She was not even surprised that he knew Clint was here. "He decided to learn all about the business," she explained, almost pleadingly. "And Clara is taking a stenographic course; and she comes in every afternoon after her class. And Inspector, they enjoy it. They really do. It's all so new to them."

There was always something in Tope's mien which could elicit confidences. "I expect they'd been running wild before," he suggested.

She did not at once reply; but he thought her shoulders drooped, as though under a heavy burden. Then they lifted again; and she said at last, in a low tone, summoning old memories:

"I knew them when they were babies. A little girl and a little boy. They were sweet children, and they began to grow up, and went to school. Of course I was just their father's secretary; but he often worked at home, and they would come into the office. . . . Then he died, and they were old enough so that they were free."

She hesitated, then went on: "I tried to—guide them. But perhaps I was not very wise. They always have—loved me, I think; but Mr. Peace encouraged them to enjoy themselves. I could not oppose him without losing their—affection. So they had too much to spend and too little to do. Clara wanted to act in moving pictures. She went to a theatrical school in California. Not with any serious ambition, I'm afraid, but rather because it promised gay amusement. Clint was studying at Beaux Arts, in Paris."

She continued reluctantly:

"And then Clara—" She seemed to choose her words.

"Clara was young," she said. "And the child is naturally affectionately, friendly. There was an older man whom she knew here. If I told you his name. . . . But that is not necessary. However, it was because of him that I did not protest when she went to California. But he followed her, or at least he too went out there, and saw a great deal of her. She went with him everywhere—not too wisely! The thing eventually ended in an ugly brawl!"

She made a weary gesture, and her voice seemed about to break, so that Inspector Tope said quickly:

"All that's over with, ma'am. You never mind about it."

She nodded. "But Clint heard about it in Paris, and started for California to kill the man!"

Tope wagged his head. "Killing is serious! I've seen a lot of it, and I don't like it," He looked toward Clint yonder and chuckled. "But that boy wouldn't. . . ."

Miss Moss set him right. She seemed to find nothing incredible in the fact that she should thus confide in a man she had never seen until today. She said: "I think Clint might have. Mr. Jervis had a furious, uncontrolled temper when his anger was aroused; a really deadly temper. Clint has it, and Clara too. I've seen it in them. Clint cabled me that he had heard about Clara, and was sailing for home on his way to California; and I was terrified, afraid of what he might do.

"And then Mr. Peace disappeared, and it seemed almost opportune. I caught Clint on the boat by radio, and wired Clara what had happened; and they hurried home."

The old man shifted in his chair, he said reassuringly: "I've a notion the Jervis Trust will be back on its feet again, by the time these young ones get some idea what money's for. Don't you think so?"

He saw her throat work as she tried to speak; but she made no sound. And he said then, in an urgent tone:

"Ma'am, I don't care anything about Peace. But I hate to see that much money get away. I thought we might do something about that, in a quiet way. You and me."

She whispered: "They don't need more money than they have. They've never been so happy as they are right now."

He saw her trembling; and he protested: "You don't have

to be upset. If you say it's best this way, that's the way it's going to be."

"You won't—do anything?"

"You're going to keep right on running the Jervis family, for all of me," he assured her. "Only—I might give you a hand!"

And she sat very still, as though relief flowed through her; and he spoke casually, of matters familiar to them both, so that she might become composed again.

"Mr. Peace played it pretty safe," he remarked. "That was why he came in to see you, pretending to be this Burke. If you recognized him, he could pass it off for a joke; but when you didn't know him—or didn't let on—he'd figured it was safe to go ahead."

"I didn't understand, at the time," she told him. "I just thought it was a prank, a jest."

He saw she was once more mistress of herself, and he spoke more gravely. "But ma'am," he insisted, "this sort of thing, it doesn't just happen and then end. There's a lot of money mixed up in it. That money has been stolen once, and money that's been stolen once—excuse me, ma'am—is like a woman that's had a lover. Men are bound to look at it sidewise, soon as they know. Scheming how to get a share.

"I've seen killings that were done for a lot less than that," he continued. "You and me, we ought not to let it lie around loose. Someone will find out Peace has got it, and kill him and take it; or he'll kill someone to keep it. I'd feel a sight easier if the bonds were back in your safe downstairs."

"Mr. Peace is clever," she said, half to herself. "No one will recognize him unless he wishes them to. I have seen him go to a masquerade without a mask, and remain unknown as long as he chose."

"He can't do things alone, all the time," Tope urged. "I'm betting right now that there's someone knows where he is, and what he looks like. . . . Maybe a woman!"

"He would not trust any woman," she declared.

Tope said slowly: "This is all guesswork. But I'm guessing that Mr. Peace didn't get hurt as bad as he pretended, in that smash-up two years ago. I'm guessing that his feet are as sound as mine. And I'm doubting about that scar on his head."

"How could he have pretended that?" she protested; and Tope hesitated, and then he chuckled.

"Why ma'am, I'm talking too much," he admitted. "But it's easy to talk to you. He might not have been hurt at all. You see, the doctor that took care of him was a friend of Peace's; and he wasn't much of a doctor either. He didn't have a real high-class reputation. I looked him up. He's retired now, moved away. Canter was his name."

He was watching her, so that he saw her head, in silhouette against the light behind, move convulsively as though with deep surprise. But before he could speak, there was an interruption. The door behind them opened, over across the room; and someone called:

"Hullo, folks!" Then, doubtfully: "Oh!"

Tope turned; and he saw a girl standing there just within the door, and he knew this must be Clara Jervis. A fair, tall girl with laughing eyes, in which for all their friendly mirth the shadow of a stale hurt still did well. Tope had expected to see sophistication, recklessness, audacity. But this girl was as wholesome as a red apple in the sun. She came across the room, stripping off her gloves, to greet Miss Moss; and young Clint drew toward them, and Tope saw old Beede watch them both with affectionately twinkling eyes.

Miss Moss introduced these two young people to the Inspector. "Clint, Clara, this is Inspector Tope," she said. "Inspector Howell asked his help in locating Mr. Peace, and they found him, but he got away."

"Found him?" young Clint ejaculated. "Where?"

Miss Moss looked at Tope; and so did they; and the old man said mildly:

"Why, he'd been sitting tight, waiting for the hunt to quiet down. Even a rabbit knows that the way to keep out of sight is to stay still. Mr. Peace just moved downstairs into the cellar, in the apartment house where he lived. He went to work as the janitor there. Then today Inspector Howell figured out where he was, and went to get him. But he'd gone."

Clint said shrewdly: "I expect you had something to do

with Inspector Howell's finding him, didn't you? Howell's been chasing his own tail like a kitten for so long!"

Tope chuckled at the thought of comparing big Dave Howell to a kitten; but he had no need to reply, for Clara cried:

"The janitor! Why, for mercy's sake, I must have talked to him! There was a tap dripping in my bathroom, and I telephoned down, two or three days ago, to the superintendent. He wasn't there, but a man who said he was the janitor answered; said he'd see to it."

Tope asked, interested: "You live in that same apartment, do you?"

"We all do," Clara assured him; and Miss Moss explained:

"Mr. Jervis kept one suite for his own use there. He arranged that it should always be reserved for the children. Rather than let it stand empty, I've lived there while they were away; and Clint and Clara came there too, when they came home, and insisted that I stay."

Clara cried affectionately: "Of course we did."

And Tope asked: "See this janitor, did you?"

"No," Clara confessed. "I was gone before he came upstairs."

Tope nodded. "Nobody ever sees a janitor," he agreed. "I guess Mr. Peace remembered that, when he figured where to hide."

"But his voice didn't sound the same," Clara protested. "I'd have known Mr. Peace's voice, I'm sure. It was different, high and reedy." She spoke to Inspector Tope, her eyes dancing. "I should think you policemen would feel a little bit foolish," she laughingly declared. "Letting him get away!"

Tope chuckled; and Miss Moss said, defending him: "Inspector Tope is retired, Clara. He's not a policeman any more. Just a friend of Inspector Howell's."

Clara said contritely: "Oh, sorry! I didn't hurt your feelings, did I?"

"Well, nobody can blame you folks," Tope admitted, "for wondering why the police didn't get him."

But Clint spoke reassuringly: "Not a bit of it. Matter of

fact, I blame myself. I ought to have been on the job here. I was supposed to take a hand in running things here when I was twenty-five, a year ago. But I let it slide. My own fault, if it's anybody's." He added: "But I don't give a hoot about the money. Neither does Clara! We've having more fun right now than we ever had before. Only I hate to have anyone put it over on us this way!"

Tope glanced at Miss Moss, who watched these two so tenderly; and he said: "I feel the same!" He chuckled. "Point of honor," he suggested. "Or habit. A policeman hates to see a criminal get away."

Clara said gaily: "You don't seem at all like a policeman. I've always wanted to know one. Unofficially." The Inspector caught again that faint shadow in her eyes as though she winced with some almost forgotten pain. "I don't mean traffic cops, of course; but real policemen, the ones who catch thieves and murderers and people like that." And as though her own words reminded her, she turned quickly to Miss Moss. "Oh, I saw Mat this afternoon, darling," she reported. "He wants Clint and me to have dinner with him tonight. Kay Ransom will be there. Why don't you come, too?"

Inspector Tope saw that she had for a moment forgotten him; and he found himself absurdly wishing that these folk would not forget him. He liked them, he liked Miss Moss; and he was sometimes a lonely old man. He asked:

"Miss Ransom? That's the young lady in the play at the Booth, isn't it? I saw it last night."

"Of course," Clara assented. "And Mat Hews. He's in it, too. I knew him in California, you see. Clint and I just keep going to see the show. I've been trying to persuade Miss Moss to go with us. You tell her she must. Do!"

She seemed to discover in Inspector Tope's eyes at this suggestion something which amused her; for she insisted:

"Do! Please! I know she will if you tell her to!" Her eyes were twinkling with a sober mirth.

But before Tope could reply, Clint asked: "What did you think of the play, Inspector?"

Tope chuckled. "Young friend of mine asked me the same thing, yesterday," he remembered. "He wrote up a long interview about it for the Sunday paper. I don't know as I ever met criminals just like the ones in that play; but maybe there are some!"

"But isn't it thrilling?" Clara insisted. "Doesn't it make the chills run up and down your spine?"

Tope's eyes were smiling. "Why, I guess my spine isn't much of a race track for chills, Miss," he said gravely. "I don't know as I've been what you might call excited for a good many years now. Don't know as I recollect when I was excited the last time, for the matter of that." The old man was not usually so talkative, nor so free to talk about himself; he was suddenly conscious of this, and he added apologetically: "I can see how it might, some people, though."

Clara exclaimed: "Of course you must have seen the most fearful things!" Her eyes were round and still with interest. "Have you always been a policeman?" she asked.

He said gently: "I quit being one, a year or two ago." His eyes met those of Miss Moss for a moment, with something like a smile in them; and he saw faint color touch her cheeks.

"Did you catch a lot of burglars and murderers and things?" the girl insisted; and Tope felt a warm pleasure at her questionings.

"Why, murderers were my specialty," he confessed. "I was the homicide man at Headquarters for quite a while."

"Homicide? That is murder, isn't it?" the girl echoed. "Do they have special policemen for special things that way?" And when he assured her this was to some extent the case, she said eagerly: "Oh, but I want to ask you millions of questions. You must tell me hundreds of stories, about all the murderers you've caught!" She appealed to these others. "Clint. Miss Moss. Don't let him go away! Do you realize that he knows all the mystery stories himself? He's been in them!" Her eyes lighted with abrupt inspiration. "I know! We'll all have dinner together, with Mat and Kay. Mat will want to meet you, Inspector; and you'll like him." Her cheeks were bright. "He's a peach, honestly! And we'll make Miss Moss go along, and we'll go to the show afterward. You must be her beau, Inspector!" She looked at the older woman with quick laughter. "Darling, you're blushing!" she cried. "The idea!" Her own enthusiasm swept her on. "But you wouldn't be afraid, with the Inspector there to take care of you!"

Miss Moss said gently: "It's a long time since I've been afraid of anything on my own account, child!"

"Then it's settled!" Clara cried. "Inspector, you'll come! I'll telephone Mat to meet us at the Touraine at six. He and Kay have to be at the theatre by seven-thirty, you know. . . ."

"You'll hardly get seats for tonight," Inspector Tope suggested, but she said:

"Oh, Mat reserves some good seats for every night, right up to the last minute, in case friends of his want them. He'll take care of us." And she caught up the telephone, called a number. While she waited, she watched them over her shoulder. "Don't move!" she insisted gaily. "I'm going to keep my eye on you. You shan't get away. . . ."

Inspector Tope stood smiling while they all listened to her one-sided conversation with young Mat Hews: "Mat? Yes, it's me, of course . . . Do so many girls call you up you can't be sure. . . . Darling, the most gorgeous news. We're all coming to dinner, the Touraine grill, six o'clock. And I'm bringing the most amazing man. He's a policeman, a regular Sherlock Holmes. He's caught hundreds of murderers, and he'll tell stories till your hair stands on end. . . . Yes, of course. Inspector Tope. . . . You have? Well, I know he is. Tell Kay she'll be mad about him. But she'll have to be careful of Miss Moss. . . ." Her eyes were dancing. "Right, darling! Six, in the grill. And we're going to the show afterward. Four of us! Can you get extra tickets? That's grand! At six, then. 'Bye!"

She swung back to them. "There. . . ."

Clint, watching the Inspector, saw the old man's faint confusion; and he said reassuringly: "Clara will chatter you black in the face, but she's a nice kid, Inspector. Don't let her rattle you. Of course, we're all anxious to have you come along, if you can!"

Inspector Tope looked at Miss Moss, almost appealingly. The old man did want to come along. There was something friendly and wholly delightful about these young folk; something deeply reassuring in the older woman. He would be sorry not to see them all again. He looked at Miss Moss as though for permission; and he asked at last doubtfully:

"Do you agree with all these plans, ma'am?"

She said immediately: "Yes; I do hope you can join us."

"Why, I'd like to," he answered instantly.

And Clara cried: "But it's all arranged! I'll have to go home first. Clint, will you drive me out? And we'll meet at six. Miss Moss, are you ready to go home?"

Miss Moss said evasively: "I've half an hour here, still. Some small matters. . . . The Inspector and I. . . ."

"Don't let him escape!" Clara urged. "I'm leaving him in your hands. Clint, we've got to race. Till six, then. Good-bye, everybody."

So she and Clint departed, and it was as though a summer breeze blew out of the dingy offices when they were gone, and left a musty silence behind. Old Beede had already hung up his black alpaca coat and his eye shade, and packed up his ledgers and taken himself away. Miss Moss and the Inspector were left alone.

The Inspector stayed, because there was still a question in his mind. The old man had an instinct, long developed, upon which he had learned to rely. Great surgeons have a similar gift, born of experience. They may know a thing without being able to say how they know. Here are two persons deathly ill; the surgeon looks upon one and says: "He will get better." And of the other: "He will die!" He can give no clear and cogent reason for the differences in his opinion; yet his judgment will prove accurate, all the same. It was so with Tope. Without knowing how he knew certain things, he nevertheless knew them certainly enough.

Thus now he knew, without knowing how, that this matter was not ended. Peace was gone, and barring the chance that Dave Howell might overtake his quarry, the incident was closed. Yet Tope was sure that there was more to come. He sought now, in a groping fashion, to discover some fact which would justify his premonition; which would serve to support the conviction that rested as yet upon instinct alone.

When Clint and Clara had disappeared, the old man said:

"They're fine children." He added, half to himself: "It's

hard to believe a girl like that would get mixed up in—the sort of thing you mentioned."

She explained carefully: "Clara is enthusiastic, ebullient, and—young. Also, I think she had quarrelled with Mat Hews at the time, wanted to punish him. They're devoted, you know!" The Inspector smiled; and she continued: "The thing was not serious, except for its consequences. Clara went with the man to an Inn in the mountains for dinner, and bad weather caught them, and snow made the roads impassable, so that they had to stay overnight. Some other woman followed him up there in spite of the snow, and tried to shoot him; and the whole affair found its way into the papers, and the man told a reporter that their trip into the mountains was Clara's suggestion!" She hesitated, said precisely: "I believe he resented the fact that Clara had rebuffed him. This was his gesture of revenge!"

"Nice fellow!" Tope commented in a dry tone.

"So Mat thrashed him rather thoroughly," Miss Moss explained. "And Clint started home to kill him. He might have done so—but for this other thing."

Tope nodded, and he rose. Yet he hesitated, conscious that there was something elusive in the background of his mind. He said awkwardly:

"I'd like to fetch you, later, if I may."

"I'll come with the children," she assured him, smiling. "You mustn't take Clara's jokes too seriously, Inspector!"

He chuckled. "Why, ma'am," he declared, "that was my own idea! But if there's no need. . . ." He turned toward the door; but halfway across the room he paused, and he came back toward her. He stood looking down at her, assorting his impressions, till she asked at last:

"What is it, Inspector?"

Tope said carefully: "I just remembered! Before she came, a while ago, we were talking about Peace, and how he could fake that scar, and the crippled foot, and I told you his doctor was a friend of his by the name of Canter. And you kind of jumped, as if you'd heard of Doctor Canter. And then Miss Jervis came in, before I could ask you. . . ."

Miss Moss was like stone; and he spoke directly. "Had you, ma'am?" he asked. "Had you heard of him?"

For a long moment she did not reply. But she said at last, as though this coincidence could puzzle her: "Yes! I had forgotten he was Mr. Peace's doctor until you spoke of it; but he was the man who—was involved with Clara, in California!"

Tope wiped his mouth with his hand. His head wagged almost contentedly; he nodded with a cheerful relief.

"Ma'am," he said, "that's fine!"

"What do you mean?" she asked.

He hesitated. "I don't want to scare you," he told her. "I guess you don't scare easy. But an old fire horse can hear a bell a long ways. I've had an itching feeling that this business wasn't done; and I didn't know why. I don't know now! But this Doctor Canter has been in it twice already; and I'm guessing he'll turn up again! It kind of relieves me. It makes things fit, someway!"

She asked gravely: "What do you mean? How?"

Tope shook his head. "I don't know, ma'am. I said I'm guessing; but it's not even a guess. Just a—feeling!" He looked toward the door through which Clint and Clara had gone. "I don't know anything," he said in a perturbed tone. "But if you'll let me, till the whole book's closed, I'd like mightily to stand by!"

She did not answer, and he urged: "It's them I'm thinking of. You mind if I stay around?"

"I wish you would," she said then slowly. "I've been—alone—taking care of them, so long."

4

When Inspector Tope left Miss Moss at the offices of the Jervis Trust, he went directly back to his own room; and his thoughts were intent upon these children, and upon Miss Moss who tended them. The old man had an audacity of his own; he could recognize and appreciate this quality in others. This woman, hiding the still passion of her devotion beneath an exterior like iron, willing to flout the law and put her own liberty at stake for the sake of the children she loved, appealed to him with an astonishing intensity. She was so calm and so serene; yet beneath the mirror surface which she wore such turbulent currents flowed. . . .

He chose to walk home, striding down Tremont Street at that characteristic gait, his hands swinging, the palms forward; and he smiled at his thoughts, and his eyes were beaming. It was one of those warm winter evenings when spring seems not far away. The dusky sky was a pale and pulsing blue, delicate and warm; the street lights were yellow jewels gleaming in the still lingering light of day.

He was thinking of Miss Moss, but not at all of Peace; so when he saw, a block ahead of him, looming bulkily among the scattered pedestrians, the heavy figure of Dave Howell, he had a guilty impulse to turn aside and avoid the other man. For Dave, after all, was intent on finding Peace, and Miss Moss had let the embezzler get away, and Tope approved her courses. But before he could escape, he and the other man came face to face; and Dave said morosely:

"Hello, Inspector!"

Tope smiled amiably. "Hello, Dave," he returned. "Got Peace already, have you?"

Howell shook his head. "But he can't get away," he said. "I know what he looks like, now. Thin, and gray hair, and a scrubby beard. And no more limp than a fish!"

"He'd change that," Tope suggested. "He probably had a room in a boarding house somewhere. He'd go there and change his clothes, change his looks. Peace won't leave town yet!"

"What's to keep him?" Howell objected; and Tope said thoughtfully:

"He'll be watching his back track to find out whether you're hot on the trail. Michelsen heard from him since he left, has he?"

"I haven't seen Michelsen."

"Let's find out," Tope proposed; and they turned into the subway station to a telephone. Howell called Michelsen; and when he came out of the booth, his eyes were bright.

"You're six jumps ahead of a kangaroo, old man," he said admiringly. "Burke—that's Peace—did telephone Michelsen, half an hour ago, asking if anyone had come to look for him. The Swede told him I'd been there. I'll trace the call. . . ."

Tope wagged his head. "Don't waste your time," he urged, frowning with a slow perplexity.

Howell made an explosive sound: "What do you want me to do; stand here and watch the crowd go by?"

Tope was thinking aloud. "Peace is a gamester, Dave," he said. "He's playing a game right now, for the fun of it. You ever play hide-and-seek when you were young? Remember how when you got a good hiding place, and they didn't find you, you stood it as long as you could, and then you'd give some sign? Whistle, or hoot, or something? At first you wanted not to be found; but there wasn't any fun in that if they never looked in your direction at all. Peace is going to be in that frame of mind pretty soon, wanting you to look right in his direction without seeing him!"

And he considered; and Howell asked angrily: "What good does that do me?"

"It's just like hide-and-seek," Tope insisted. "If the boy who was It didn't find you, you were always itching to give him a signal. And if you were It and couldn't find anyone, the best way was to get out of sight yourself, and wait till someone stuck out his head to see where you were. You might try that. Keep out of sight till he thinks you've gone away!"

But these psychological abstractions were beyond the comprehension of big Dave Howell. He said as much. "The only way I know to hunt for a man is to hunt for him," he insisted angrily; and he asked: "Had dinner? Where you bound now?"

Tope chuckled. "I'm stepping out, Dave," he confessed. "I went back to the Jervis Trust after you phoned me. Did you know young Clint is home, and his sister too? That was Clint we saw up there, in Randall's place. He's gone to work for a living. I'm having dinner with them all tonight."

"The kid's home?" Howell exclaimed. "Those wild cubs!"

"They're taming down," Tope assured him. "Miss Moss has a head on her shoulders. She'll handle them yet—if they don't have too much money for a while."

And he went on, willing in fairness to give Dave a chance to guess the truth: "I don't think she's sorry Peace got away.

I believe she thinks they're better off without the money. She's mothered them since they were babies! You know the way a spinster will take another woman's children into her heart, make them her own."

"I guess they'll take the money if we find it, just the same," Howell said grimly.

Tope assented. "Yes." His eyes clouded. "And that might be bad!" He looked at Howell, and he added slowly: "I've one of my hunches, Dave. This show isn't over. There's trouble coming still."

"There's always trouble," Dave agreed, "when four hundred thousand dollars gets out of the pasture, till it's back behind the bars again."

And after another word or two, they parted and Tope went on toward the room that was his home. He had still half an hour or so before the rendezvous at the Touraine; he shaved and changed. Evening clothes, it occurred to him, might be the order of the day; but the old man was not used to such regalia. He had tails packed away in camphor; he took the garments out, examined the yellowed vest, the tawny linen. But he decided in the end he were better advised to attempt nothing he could not perform. He put on a light gray suit, relatively new; and he brushed his shoes, and he had an impulse—which amused him—to buy a flower for his buttonhole. At a quarter before six, feeling as starched and uncomfortable as a boy on Sunday morning, he descended to the street and turned toward the hotel.

The Touraine grill is just below the street level, reached by elevator from the lobby or by stairs from the street. Tope descended the stairs into the corridor where coats were hung on a long rack, and cigars and cigarettes and magazines were dispensed from a convenient counter. He surrendered his coat and hat to the woman in black with a white apron who was in attendance there, and bought an evening paper and sat down to read it with the slow attention the columns of the press could always command from him; and then two young people came down in the elevator and looked up and down the corridor, and stood talking together in low tones, laughing now and then.

He recognized them readily enough; Mat Hews and Kay

Ransom. Young Hews, he thought, was not by any stretch of the term handsome; his countenance had a battered appearance, and he was lean and only moderately tall. But his eyes were gay and his mouth was firm. Kay was shorter than he, black-haired, pretty in that colorful fashion which so soon surrenders to encroaching years. When the sparkle of youth should have departed from her eyes, she would not draw a second glance from passers-by; but just now she was vivacious, charming. He watched them over his paper covertly; he heard a word or two of their casual conversation. And then Clint and Clara Jervis and Miss Moss came down the stairs together, and Mat and Kay moved quickly to meet them, and the four young people talked all at once, so that Tope had time for a moment's absurd fear that they had forgotten him before Clara discovered him sitting here behind his paper, and came swiftly across the corridor, exclaiming:

"Inspector! Waiting long? Clint's always ten minutes late. Come and meet Mat and Kay."

She was so young, he had a sudden rueful pity for her. Youth knows so little what to expect from life. It is as well for mankind, he thought, not to know the future; the weight of all the mishaps to come, if they could be foreseen, would crush even the bright valor of youth. He remembered, as he crossed toward where the others stood, that dim certainty he knew a while ago that this business of Peace was not yet done; and then Mat Hews gripped his hand, and Kay Ransom cried:

"A policeman? A murder man? Inspector, I'm thrilled!"

Then Miss Moss came to stand beside him, and he found this woman like an anchorage, calm and secure. She was at his left at the round table, Kay Ransom on his right. Clara and Mat were side by side and the Inspector saw that they were at first absorbed in one another, their voices low, their eyes joined in a warm glance.

He had expected to sustain a sort of catechism from these youngsters; he had even prepared a tale or two to tell them. But almost from the first Kay and Mat talked shop, and the others were content to listen while their swift tongues ran. Their work, he saw, possessed them completely.

Mat remembered at last to ask politely:

"You've seen the show, Inspector?" And when Tope nodded: "Hammond is great, don't you think?"

"I thought he was afraid," said Tope, rather surprised at his own words. He had not been conscious of thinking Hammond was afraid; yet in retrospect now he realized that this was in fact the case. The man, who played the part of a saturnine and dauntless criminal, had in fact worn the impalpable aura of some secret fear.

Mat assented reflectively: "That's so! I hadn't thought, but it is so!"

And Kay Ransom said with a relish: "Of course he is! You remember, when that Mrs. Dillaway died they almost indicted him, and for years and years he couldn't get any parts at all. I suppose he's always expecting something like that again."

And she talked on, and Mat put in a word now and then, and Clara too. The company had been organized in California; Clara herself had watched their first rehearsals. She knew the whole cast almost as well as Kay did. And Tope, listening, learned many things of no least importance. He heard how Hammond had built up his part, constantly adding or eliding lines, forever trying new bits of business; he heard how Mat had by accident discovered an effective gesture which he used in the murder scene; he heard how seriously Madison, the stage manager, took the fact that he was Hammond's understudy; he heard Kay's boast that it was she who had suggested the most effective business in the play, as a result of which Lola Cyr now calmly powdered her nose in that hideous moment when behind her the machine guns were chopping down four men. And the old Inspector learned that Max Urbin, who played opposite Hammond, was afraid of his wife, a withered little woman who came to the theatre for every performance to make jealously sure that he exchanged no word with Lola Cyr, or Kay. And Hammond had a new valet who was desperately in love with Lola's middle-aged French maid and trailed her hopelessly. And Lola Cyr had a new man on the string, Kay cried; but Mat Hews interrupted her in a fashion Tope thought abrupt.

He wondered if these others thought so too, but if they did, they gave no sign.

"Hammond is mad about her, Kay," Mat insisted curtly, and Kay met his eyes, and said then:

"Of course. All men are! She's mysterious, no end, my dear! She makes a fetish of it. It's good publicity for her, of course; but she certainly puts on a show. I'll hand it to her. No address, no phone, comes and goes alone. Even her make-up stuff all has the labels scraped off, so you can't find out what kind of cream she uses, or perfume. She says her private life is her own business!" The girl was suddenly a mimic, her voice a deep, throaty murmur. "Upon the stage, I belong to the world, but once the curtain falls, I belong to myself alone."

Clint drawled in an amused tone: "I wonder! They say otherwise."

"Oh, she's got the name all right," Kay agreed. "Whether she's got the game too, I don't know. She doesn't deny it! In fact, she hints at it all the time. I've talked to her." She became Lola again, her tones vibrating, almost masculine.

"Never love any man, my child, unless you know his means. Wealthy men love as ardently as poor ones, and they're so much more entertaining!"

"Advice to the lovelorn?" Clint chuckled, and Kay nodded.

"She's always giving advice, yes. I told her I was beginning to be that way about you, Clint darling! She warned me off. Told me you were probably on an allowance, hadn't a cent except what you spend."

"Right," Clint agreed. "I'm poor as a church mouse, Kay. If I endowed you with all my wordly goods, you couldn't buy half a dozen pairs of stockings. Not that I'm offering, you know!"

She made an amused grimace. "Don't be so cautious!" she derided. "Just because there are witnesses! You don't talk that way when we're alone!"

Clint flushed almost angrily; and Kay laughed, Tope thought too gaily. He had a sudden impression that there was a hard calculation in the girl. He looked at Clara wondering whether she liked Kay, and he saw that she and

Mat were holding hands under the table, oblivious to everything but each other.

Then Clint said in a dry tone: "Now you're bragging, Kay!"

And Tope, because he liked to try experiments, remarked to Miss Moss:

"Miss Cyr must have inside information about the Jervis affairs!"

There was a sudden silence, and they all looked at him, and Kay cried: "Why? Whatever do you mean?"

Miss Moss said calmly: "The trustee of the estate has run away with some securities that didn't belong to him, Miss Ransom. Clara and Clint aren't as well off as they were!"

Tope, watching her, thought she was glad of the chance to make this statement, as though she were willing to make sure that neither Mat nor Kày had any mercenary ground for the affection in which they appeared to hold Clint and Clara. There was a moment's silence and then Kay cried in shrill amusement:

"Paupers? Clint darling, that's splendid! You must go on the stage! I'll make Madison let them murder you with Mat every night, or something. I always said I'd never marry a loafer! But turn workingman, my dear, and see. . . ."

They laughed at her, and the Inspector, content with his experiment, asked curiously:

"Is it true Miss Cyr is bald, has no hair?"

Mat looked at Kay to reply. "I don't know," Kay confessed. "And I'm dying to know, too. I've never seen her without that turban thing she wears. I've heard that she hasn't a hair on her head. It must be ghastly! Can you imagine it? Just a shiny, white skull and that beautiful face of hers on the front of it."

And she added: "But she gets men, somehow! Hammond hangs around her all the time; and there's a new one back stage to see her almost every night!"

Mat said abruptly: "Kay, we've got to run!" Inspector Tope saw that the young man was ill at ease. He signalled the waiter, signed the check. "I've left tickets at the box office, Clara," he explained. "You folks sit here and finish your coffee. You've lots of time."

"We'll come back and see you after the first act," Clara promised. But Mat negatived that proposal.

"No, don't," he said positively. "Madison's shutting down on visitors. We'll meet you here for supper, if you like."

Clara laughed. "All right," she agreed. "But I'm not afraid of Madison!" And Kay protested that it was not yet time to go; but Mat insisted, led her at last away. The Inspector, watching them in the corridor outside the grill, saw that he spoke sharply to the girl, chiding her for something or other. It was Tope's ancient habit when he saw a thing he did not understand, to wonder, to seek to discover reasons why.

He had more and more, during the half hour that they sat over their coffee, the troubled sense that something did impend; that these young folk here, and Miss Moss who loved them, were in danger. Once he thought there were eyes upon him; and he looked all around, covertly, half-expecting to see someone here who might be Peace. But there was no individual in the room who could fit the embezzler's description.

He talked with Miss Moss for a while, about indifferent matters; and Clint smoked a cigarette, and Clara was quiet and at ease. Then it was time for them to go. They walked the short distance to the theatre. The streets were bright and noisy with traffic, the sidewalks crowded. Clint got their tickets at the box office while they waited in the narrow lobby; then they took their places in the file of laughing folk who were pressing toward the door.

Inspector Tope had an astonishing reluctance to go in. When he had passed the ticket taker, for no reason in the world he looked back and all around, scanning every countenance with quick and wary eyes. He had the animal's sense that this was a trap; that death was lurking here.

This play which they were tonight to witness attracted an audience distinctive and unique; it imposed upon the individuals of that audience, from the moment they entered the doors of the theatre, a new character. Suspense may be the essential element of drama; but there was here no suspense at all. The story of the play had been told and re-told, by word of mouth and by the press, till it was known in advance to every individual in the stalls. They came, not out of curiosity, but from a furtive appetite for violence; they came as the Roman throngs came to the Coliseum, to see bloody battle and stark death. They came in order that their spines might be made to congeal; and though they might have but just arisen from some festive dinner table, their voices, once they were within the theatre, were likely to hush to whispers. Laughter was smothered; each man watched his neighbor with an instinctive feeling that there might be a flat automatic pistol in the side pocket of the dinner jacket which the other wore.

After they were in their seats, the Inspector, in the brief interval before the curtain rose, took note of his surroundings, just as the driver of an automobile, approaching another car, instinctively observes the width of the road, the depth of the ditch, the possibility of turning off the highway to safety if any emergency should suddenly arise. He had once been in a theatre when smoke curled up from the orchestra pit and the thrill of panic ran across the house, and he was always since then faintly uneasy in a press of people.

But this could not account for his uneasiness tonight. He thought his feeling might arise from the tension obvious all around him; from the lowered voices, the nervous laughter, the whispering tones. Miss Moss said quietly:

"A strange audience. They whisper like conspirators."

He nodded, and he had a new respect for her acuteness because she felt this too. "They know what's coming," he explained. "Every woman in the house is wondering whether she will scream, or faint, when the shooting starts!"

"Why are they here?" she wondered. "I came because I like to be with the children, when they want me. But why have these others come?"

"To find out what it's like to see a man killed," said Tope gravely; and after a moment she smiled and confessed:

"I think I'm curious, about myself. To see what I will do."

Then the curtain slid upward with a whispering hiss; and a murmur swept across the audience as it settled into silence, and Clara beyond Miss Moss pressed closer to the older woman and Tope heard her laughing entreaty:

"Hold my hand, darling! Please!"

The Inspector was during what followed more attentive to the audience than to the play. By suggestion, by clever stagecraft, by a dozen indirections the players cast across the house a sinister spell. When there was a laugh in the lines, the laugh was hurried, as though those who laughed were impatient to hear what was to come. Or the laughter was too loud and long, as though in sheer relief to tight and jangling nerves.

The first act was clear and precise in its every implication; when the curtain fell, the groundwork had been laid for that which was to come.

The curtain fell, and the lights gleamed bright and pitiless, and folk hurried up the aisle to snatch a cigarette during the intermission. Clint and Clara rose too, and Tope and Miss Moss got up to let them pass.

"We're going back to see Mat," Clara explained.

But Miss Moss objected: "He asked you not to!"

The girl laughed: "Oh, Madison's a grouch; but he's not as bad as he pretends. Why don't you two come? You've never been behind the scenes. Do!"

Miss Moss hesitated, and she looked at Inspector Tope. He had an uncertain desire to stay near these young people; he had an absurd sense that danger threatened them. "Shall we?" he asked.

"I think not," she decided at last. "We'll wait here." She asked Clara: "Do you really think you'd better go?"

Clara gaily protested: "Of course! But we'll be back. 'Bye." And she and her brother hurried up the aisle. Tope turned to watch them. There was a door communicating with the stage, behind the boxes to the left; and he thought Clint and Clara might go that way. But they went out through the lobby, to the stage door, he supposed.

When they were gone, he sat silent for a while, remembering that when Peace disappeared it was in this theatre. And Tope wondered about this; and he thought it might be well to talk to Walter Hammond by and by, seek to get from him some small circumstance which Howell might have overlooked. Tope was not particularly anxious to locate Peace unless Miss Moss wished that this should be done; yet any enigma always vexed and goaded him till it was solved.

Then Miss Moss asked him some question about the play, and he answered her; and the folk who had gone out to smoke came drifting down the aisles; and suddenly the house was dark, the curtain rose again.

Clint and Clara had not returned. Miss Moss whispered: "Where are they?"

He looked behind them, toward the lobby. "Perhaps delayed," he suggested. "They will have to come around from the stage door; it needs a minute or two."

But they did not appear; and he and Miss Moss gave only half their attention to the stage where now the play went on.

The scene of this second act was an automobile salesroom. Mat Hews and Kay were there, just returned from lunch, laughing together. Two other salesmen, lay figures of no importance in the play, dressed the set. There was an elevator at one side; a freight elevator for lifting cars from the basement, or to the floor above. After her scene with Mat, Kay stepped into the elevator and Mat pulled at the cable and started the car slowly upward. He watched her out of sight, called: "All right?" And at her assent, he pulled the cable again and the heavy elevator came slowly down to its place at the level of the stage once more.

Tope noticed that the elevator shaft appeared to be walled with brick; and he wondered whether the bricks were real. He had heard that for greater verisimilitude, the machine guns were loaded with paper wads which spattered against these walls. Then he forgot his conjectures, for Lola Cyr was on, with Max Urbin! The house now was taut and still. The moment was approaching.

Mat spoke with them, pointing out the excellences of the car which had caught Lola's eye. She must try the driver's seat; Urbin must see the engines under the gleaming hood. The other two salesmen in the background watched smilingly.

And then four silent men came in the door. Four men, of whom three wore overcoats. Their hands were in their pockets; and there was something awkwardly bulky beneath the overcoat each wore.

The fourth man was Hammond. He spoke to Urbin.

The ensuing colloquy was brief. One of the men in overcoats approached the salesmen. Something slender and metallic protruded from the front of his coat; and they backed into the elevator. A moment later Mat Hews was there with them! Hammond and Urbin speaking; a dry triumph in Hammond's tones, truculence in those of the other man. Truculence, yet terror too.

Then Urbin, his hands in the air, backed into the elevator. He and Mat and the other two were no longer visible to the audience. Hammond spoke, and Urbin replied. His voice could be heard, even though he could not be seen. The three overcoated men stood side by side, facing the elevator. Lola was powdering her nose, her attention all focussed on the mirror in her hands. Tope remembered Kay's boast that she had devised this business.

The machine guns clattered, a fierce and deadly rattle like that of a monstrous serpent. The din continued till it seemed endless. Across the audience ran a twitching convulsion of horror; smothered cries; movements as though of pain. Miss Moss pressed her hand to her mouth.

Lola yonder was still powdering her nose!

Then there was silence, and the three men were gone, and Hammond came swift to Lola's side. Together they turned as though upon a signal; they pressed against the wall, their hands high, their backs toward the door.

And someone peered doubtfully in at the door, and a little crowd, forming and dissolving, came into existence there. Then a man in a blue coat pressed through; and somewhere above the stage, Kay screamed. She cried Mat's name. The elevator, with its grim freight invisible to the audience, began to rise out of sight. The officer shouted something and ran to stop it. Before he could do so, it was gone, and Kay's cries came ringing, piercing, full of grief and terror.

Hammond and Lola yonder had abandoned their posture of helplessness; they came toward the policeman, and Hammond said quickly:

"Three men, officer. Machine guns. This lady and I were looking at a car when they came in. . . ."

So the swift action ran. Other policemen arrived, and Hammond suggested that the lady, his companion, was near collapse. He proposed that he send her home in a taxicab, and was permitted to do so. He and Lola went off stage. . . .

It was a little later—a minute, three minutes, he could not be sure—that Tope was conscious of someone moving in the aisle on his left, behind the boxes. He turned and saw a man open the emergency exit and go quietly out. An usher hurried down the aisle, too late to intercept him; and Tope half rose from his seat, then sat down again.

But his senses were preternaturally alert from this moment on.

Clint and Clara, he remembered, had not yet returned from back stage; and he had an overpowering anxiety to know where they were. But Miss Moss was all attentive to the play, and he would not leave her here alone. He thought her unconscious that anything was amiss till she said to him suddenly:

"Inspector, something's wrong! See, they're mixed in their lines, making up speeches as they go along."

He had forgotten the play. He watched, and listened for a moment; said then abruptly:

"Hammond is supposed to be on the stage in this scene. He isn't there!"

"Why not?" she wondered.

He hesitated. "Taken ill, perhaps," he suggested guardedly. For he knew now that it was Hammond who had slipped out through the emergency exit a moment ago.

The act ended; the curtain somehow came down upon a botched and stumbling climax, and Miss Moss said uneasily: "I wish the children would come!"

Tope rose. "Shall we step outside?" he suggested. "Meet them, or find them?"

She asked acutely: "What is it? You are disturbed?"

"Not at all," he assured her.

She said: "Nonsense! What is the matter? Tell me. I am not a child!"

He hesitated, surrendered then. "Hammond went out a while ago," he confessed. "Through that door there!" He pointed. "I saw him go. I don't know why. . . ."

Then Clint and Clara came swiftly down the aisle, their

eyes shining. They tumbled into their seats, and—both talking at once—told their news.

"More excitement!" Clara whispered. "Hammond is gone! He just vanished! Madison will have to take his part in the third act. They're wild, back there. Nobody knows anything! Running around in circles. Hammond was supposed to be on for the end of the second act. They had to *ad lib* all over the place. H-sh!"

Someone had just stepped in front of the curtain to speak to the audience. A small, fat man with a bald head.

"Ladies and gentlemen," he said apologetically. "I regret to say that Mr. Hammond is suddenly indisposed. You may have remarked some confusion in the latter part of the preceding act. He was unable to go on. I must attempt to play his part in the third act." He smiled. "I'm afraid I can't equal Mr. Hammond's performance. As you observe, I do not look the part of a ruthless gangster. I beg you will let your imaginations help me as much as possible." He heard their good-humored laughter, smiled again. "Thank you," he said, and disappeared.

"That's Madison," Clara whispered. "And Hammond isn't sick! He's just gone! His valet said he went in to Lola's dressing room with her, but nobody saw him come out at all."

Tope asked quietly: "His hat and coat?" The man who went out through the emergency exit a while before wore a hat pulled low, a coat about his ears.

"They're in his dressing room," Clint explained.

"But why should he disappear?" Miss Moss asked. "Without any explanation?" She looked at the Inspector, hesitated, seemed about to speak; and he nodded, and she said then: "Inspector Tope saw him go out of the exit there, a while ago."

"You did?" Clara exclaimed. And Clint cried:

"Sure it was him?"

"He had a hat and coat on!" Tope confessed. "But—yes, I was sure!"

They sat in an astonished silence for a moment; and then Miss Moss spoke. She asked quietly:

"Did Miss Cyr have a caller between the acts?"

Tope moved like a man touched by an electric needle. His quick, searching mind had been groping toward this same question; hers was ahead of him. He looked at Miss Moss with a deep respect. And at the same time he realized that Clara and Clint were silent; that their eyes had met as though in startled consultation. He saw Clara faintly shake her head; but Clint said, with a slow reluctance:

"Yes, she had a caller!"

Tope said soberly: "Hammond wore an overcoat too big for him. The hat too."

And Miss Moss asked Clint: "Was this man larger than Mr. Hammond?"

But Clara whispered: "Hush, there's the curtain!"

Tope was glad for the interval that followed; for the chance to think his own thoughts while those about him were attentive to the action on the stage. It was an old habit with the man not to seek to find out too much, too rapidly; he preferred to digest first those things already known. Yet one question waited to be asked. Where was Miss Cyr's caller now; and had he missed his overcoat and hat?

Lola herself was yonder on the stage, composed, seductive, arrogantly beautiful. She wore a faintly mocking smile for Madison, short and plump and bald, was perspiring heavily in his role of her gangster lover. He knew the lines well enough; but he could only stumble through them. She embraced him, as the scene demanded; but she laughed over his shoulder at the audience. She even winked, as though to share the jest with them. The third act could be no more than a hollow burlesque, with Hammond gone. The audience began to chuckle; and the actors were quick to respond, quick to strike this key which pleased their auditors. They burlesqued the lines more and more broadly. What had been stark and stirring tragedy became broad comedy and nothing more. When Lola at last was dragged away to the cell that waited for her, and there remained only a dozen lines of the act, the house was roaring with amusement.

Lola went off stage; Madison, and the District Attorney, and an officer or two were left to speak the concluding lines.

And then the comedy ended; for from somewhere behind

the scenes there came a long, strangling cry, the hideous shriek of a human being in abject terror or pain.

Feet pounded, behind the back drop; and the sound of excited voices penetrated through the painted canvas. The actors on the stage forgot their lines to listen. And Madison made some sign to the wings, rang the curtain down.

The folk in the audience were on their feet, all attention now. Someone climbed on his seat the better to see. No one made any move to go. And Miss Moss asked Inspector Tope:

"What has happened?"

Inspector Tope said in a low tone: "I'll find out. Wait here, please. All of you."

She nodded; and he hurried up the aisle. He came around the back of the house and down by the side aisle to that door behind the boxes through which Hammond must have escaped. An usher stopped him; but Tope said calmly:

"Police Inspector Tope! Show me the way."

"Come on," the usher agreed. "They've telephoned for the police."

He opened the small door, and the Inspector passed through. . . .

He came back to rejoin the others as quickly as possible, and his eyes were intent and sombre now. But he had no need to bear the news to them; for as he approached down the aisle, Madison stepped through the curtains to say another word. The packed house listened breathlessly.

"Ladies and gentlemen," he announced. "The police request me to explain to you that there has been an—accident in one of the dressing rooms. It is suggested that you all remain for the present where you are. It will not be long. I thank you."

A man shouted: "You mean we can't get out?"

But Madison, with only a gesture for reply, turned and disappeared. Then Tope, who had paused in the aisle while Madison was speaking, came to his seat again, and Miss Moss looked up at him.

"An accident?" she asked incredulously.

"A murder!" he replied.

He saw that Clint and Clara were clinging to one another, white and still.

5

THE audience milled and murmured all about them; the aisles were filled; there was a clamor in the air, and shrill hysteria, and angry truculence, and someone in the rear of the house called in hoarse authority:

"Get back there! No! You'll have to wait a minute, please. . . ."

No accident, but murder! This was the word Inspector Tope brought from back stage; and he saw that beyond Miss Moss, Clint and Clara were rigid and pale, looking straight ahead. Then Clint whispered something to the girl; and he caught Tope's eye upon them and tried to grin. And Miss Moss smoothed down her dress precisely, and adjusted her hat upon her head, and tugged on her gloves.

"Who was it?" she asked calmly. "Who was killed?"

The Inspector shook his head. "Some man who came to see Miss Cyr," he explained. "I did not hear his name! They found his body in her dressing room."

She said composedly: "I expect it was his hat and overcoat which Mr. Hammond wore." And she asked: "Would you mind going back there again, to find out exactly what it is that has happened?" She looked at him calmly. "I'm afraid," she pointed out, "that Clint and Clara will be involved. They were back there during the second act. It may have been done then."

He could still be astonished at her strength and poise. He said honestly: "Yes." And he rose, and he was suddenly at his ease. "I want to go," he confessed. "I'm like a fire horse who hears the gong! Such matters were my business for so many years. Yes, I will go."

She predicted, as much to herself as to him: "They will start by accusing Hammond, since he ran away. But he had nothing to do with it, no part in it."

The Inspector asked: "Why? How can you know?"

"If he had done it, he would stay."

"Then why did he run away?"

"For some other reason," she urged. "Some sudden panic! Flight is terror, not confession. He was afraid; so he must have known it had happened. That is why he ran away."

Inspector Tope wagged his head. "I see," he assented. "That is so, of course." And he said, almost smilingly: "You and I would have accomplished many things together, in my old days, Miss Moss. I could recognize facts, and cling to them. But you go behind facts; go deeper." He chuckled. "Hagan should talk to you. You could help the man."

He stepped into the aisle: "Shall I come back here, or wait till tomorrow to see you again?"

"Here," she said. "We will stay till you come."

While they thus spoke together in low tones, isolated by the turmoil and the babble of the audience all about them, Clint and Clara had been obliviously whispering together. But when Tope rose now they looked up at him; and as he started to move away Clint asked sharply:

"Where are you going?"

But Tope left it to Miss Moss to answer. He threaded and elbowed his way up the aisle. The rear part of the house was crowded with people standing between the seats, and in the aisle; but from the front rows the spectators had withdrawn, as folk press back from a conflagration, as though they feared that from behind the silent curtain an explosive violence might emerge to their destruction. Tope made his way past them all; he followed the side aisle behind the boxes and opened the door to the stage.

A policeman in uniform was on guard there; a tall, rawboned traffic officer from the nearest corner, impressed for this emergency. His name was Jim Dunning, and Tope knew him of old. "Evening, Jim?" he said. "How's the missus? And that boy of yours?"

The officer grinned. "You, is it, Inspector? And they're fine! Might have known you'd turn up here."

"I was in the house," said Tope. And he asked: "Has Hagan come?"

"He's over there on the stage," Dunning pointed out, so Tope looked around. The third act set had been struck; the great stage all was bare. One huge, naked bulb hanging from overhead shed a bald illumination on the scene. And Tope took time to appraise his surroundings with a judicial eye.

The space—it was too large to be called a room—in which he now stood, extended for the full width of the auditorium; and it was roughly rectangular, save that there were projections here and there. Overhead, high in the shadows, hung drops and flats that could be lowered as they were required. Other sections of scenery were leaned against the solid wall on his left, and beyond them he saw wide, high, double doors that must admit to the alleyway outside. On his right, the curtain took the place of wall; and he could hear, muffled by its folds, the hoarse murmur of the penned crowd outside. Diagonally across from where he stood there was a doorway that admitted to a hall and to steps that must lead down to the stage door. Iron stairs ascended on the left of these steps; there was a dressing room on the right; and two other dressing rooms were built out from the rear wall, their doorways facing the curtain, with a space between where the properties and furniture required for this play were just now heaped in an orderly disarray. Tope saw there the restaurant tables from the first act; the sections of wall which formed the elevator shaft in the second act; he marked the trap cut in the floor, which when raised by mechanical lifts in the basement would serve as the elevator itself. . . . And many other things he saw.

And many people, clustered in small groups here and there. Some were old friends; some he recognized as members of the cast; some he had never seen before. Inspector Hagan, who had succeeded Tope himself in charge of murder cases, stood exactly under the bulb in the middle of the stage, his glance darting to and fro. He was talking with Madison, the fat little stage manager; and Kay Ransom stood almost between them, looking up first at one and then at the other, with quick, birdlike movements, as they spoke. Mat Hews was near them, likewise listening; and with him in a little group, Max Urbin who played the heavy role opposite Hammond in the play, and two or three of the lesser characters.

There were other men about. Some were manifestly stage

hands or the like. A group of two or three men stood yonder in the doorway to the hall. Besides Dunning, the traffic officer, there were other policemen here. One of them leaned against the wall beside the starred door of the nearer dressing room. This was Lola's, Tope understood, where the body had been found. He wondered who occupied the dressing room beyond, diagonally opposite where he stood. Its door was open, and he caught a glimpse of a man inside. The man was hanging a pair of trousers on a hook, and Tope guessed that it was Hammond's room. The little man was no doubt Hammond's valet; and he remembered that the valet, according to Kay Ransom, was hopelessly in love with Lola Cyr's maid, and smiled to himself at the thought.

Lola herself was not in sight, nor was her maid. Tope looked for them in vain.

Inspector Tope had caught Hagan's eye when he came in; and Hagan nodded to him then. But the man was still engaged with Madison, and there were things Tope wished to know. So he spoke to Dunning, here at his side, indicating the guarded door of the nearer dressing room.

"That where it happened?" he asked.

"In there," Dunning agreed. "Her dressing room. This Lola Cyr!"

"Where is she?"

"She threw a fit," said Dunning cheerfully. "Passed out cold!"

"I heard her scream!" Tope assented. "We heard that, out front."

"They've got her in Miss Ransom's dressing room," Dunning explained. "Her maid's taking care of her. She's all shot!"

Tope nodded; and then he caught Inspector Hagan's eye again, and left Dunning and walked that way.

"Hello, Tope," Hagan said. "How are you? Haven't seen you for weeks. Might have known you'd be around. . . ."

There was friendliness in his tones, but also a faint and jealous resentment too. Since he had succeeded Tope in charge of homicide, he was always conscious of the silent comparison between his work and that of his predecessor which went on in the minds of his superiors. Inspector Tope was one of those outstanding figures who now and then emerge from the multitude; a hard man to follow without suffering by contrast. Yet Hagan respected Tope, and Tope liked the younger man.

"You're on the job quick, Inspector," he commented.

"How did you hear about it?" Hagan asked.

"I was in the house," Tope explained. Madison stood by, his eyes turning from one of them to the other as they talked. The man's bald head was streaming; and the make-up he had worn when he took Hammond's part was streaked and smeared across his cheeks.

"How did it look from the front?" Hagan asked; and Tope said carefully:

"Near the end of the second act, I saw a man come out through the door behind the boxes, and go through the emergency exit into the alley, near our seats. I thought it was Hammond, had a hunch then that something was wrong. Then when the woman screamed, just before the last curtain, the audience got as nervous as though they'd smelled smoke. I was with some people, and I left them and came back to find out what had happened." He asked: "What have you got so far?"

Hagan looked around. They were encircled by listeners; but at Hagan's scowls these folk drew back; and the Inspector spoke in lowered tones.

"This man came to call on Lola Cyr," he said. "He'd been around several times lately. Never gave a name at the door. She'd leave word he was expected. He came in tonight, and went to her dressing room, after the first act. The door man let him in." He hesitated, looked around for the stage manager. "Where's that door man, Madison?" he asked harshly.

Madison made a gesture, turned hurriedly away.

"I haven't looked him over yet, except to see that he was shot at close range," Hagan explained. "Doc Gero is due here any time; thought I'd wait for him."

"You don't know who he was?" Tope asked; and Hagan shook his head. Then Madison returned with someone; he said huskily:

"Here's Peterson! He was on the door."

Peterson was an old man, slight, gray, with a thin gray

beard. He spoke in a curt, harsh tone; the tone of one used to administering rebuffs, revelling in a certain authority over folk more important than himself. And Hagan questioned him crisply:

"You on the door?"

"Yes."

"On the job tonight?"

"Since half-past six."

"All the time?"

"Yes. Only a minute or two now and then, to go downstairs, or carry a note or something."

"How many times did you leave the door?"

"I could count up, but I kept an eye on the door all the time. Nobody come in I didn't see."

"Sure?" Hagan challenged; and Peterson said angrily:

"That's my job, being sure."

Hagan said: "Don't get funny! It's my job to ask questions. You answer them. All right, you see this man when he came in?"

"Sure. Miss Cyr told me he was coming; said send him in. He'd been here before."

"Know his name?"

"No."

"When did he come?"

"Middle of the first intermission."

"You bring him in?"

"He knew the way," Peterson explained. "I told him to go ahead."

"See where he went?"

"Didn't look to see."

Hagan nodded. "Anybody else come back tonight?"

"Sure. There's always some."

The Inspector looked at Madison. "You run a pink tea back here?" he asked in a sardonic tone.

"We try to keep visitors down to a minimum," the stage manager protested. "But you can't keep 'em all out. There'd be an argument, all the time."

And Hagan turned back to the doorman again: "Many of them tonight?"

"The Jervis girl, and a young fellow. Her brother, I guess," said Peterson.

"What Jervis girl?" Hagan asked. He looked at Madison again; and before Tope could speak, Madison explained:

"Clara Jervis. She was out in California while we were rehearsing. She and young Hews, our juvenile, were in school together in Pasadena. Her brother's name is Clint. The two of them have come back stage to see Mat and Miss Ransom, half a dozen times."

"She an actress?" Hagan asked; and Madison said, with a faint smile:

"She thinks so! Wants to be!"

Tope had stood silently by; but it seemed time now to speak. He coughed faintly, and he said: "I know them, Hagan. In fact, I was with them tonight." He hesitated, then made a sign with his head and moved aside, and Hagan followed him. When they were out of hearing, Tope explained:

"You know them, too. Know who they are. This Clarence Peace that Dave Howell has been after for the last two months—he was trustee of their money, the Jervis Trust, estate of Dana Jervis. Howell came to me about it, and he and I went up to the Trust offices today. There was a woman in charge there named Moss, Miss Moss; sort of a secretary. She and the young ones and I had dinner tonight with this Mat Hews and Kay Ransom. Then we came to the show."

And before Hagan could speak, he added: "And—this may figure in what's happened here tonight. Howell found out today where Peace was hiding out; but before he could get there, Peace made a getaway."

But Hagan made an impatient gesture. "That's Howell's affair, not mine," he said, and he asked: "Did you come back stage with these kids tonight?"

Tope shook his head. "Miss Moss and I stayed out front," he explained. "The children came back after the first act, and stayed through the second act. Then they joined us again, told us about Hammond being gone."

"I'll want to talk to them," Hagan commented. "They might know something."

"They might," Tope agreed. He hesitated, half-minded to insist again that between this killing and that matter of the embezzlement from the estate some connection might lie. But this was no more than a guess on his part; and Hagan was as well entitled to guess as he. So he held his tongue on this point; added only:

"They're waiting out in front for me."

Hagan considered, and he nodded to Madison, who stood a little to one side. Madison drew near; and Hagan asked: "Anyone else back stage tonight except these three, this dead man and the two kids?"

"Only those of us had business here," Madison replied. "At least, that's what Peterson says."

"Could anyone else have come back without being seen?" Hagan insisted. "How about that door over there?" He pointed to the way by which Tope had come.

"It was bolted," Madison explained.

"Hammond skipped that way! Inspector Tope saw him go."

"He could have slipped the bolt," the stage manager explained; and Tope added:

"And the killing was done by that time, Hagan. It must have been done while the guns were going on the stage, and Hammond was on himself then, so he didn't do it."

"Then why did he take it on the run?" Hagan protested.

"I think he knew it had happened," said Tope.

Hagan considered, speaking half to himself: "Guess there's no use to hold that audience any longer. But Tope, will you ask your friends to wait? Madison, you can tell the rest of them to go."

Tope nodded his assent and moved briskly toward the door. He saw Madison wiping his brow, his bald head; ordering his collar and tie before facing the eyes of the audience. The old man passed behind the boxes and came to where Clint and Clara and Miss Moss were sitting; and as he joined them, Madison came before the curtain and made his apologetic announcement. The murmuring crowd began to press in a great relief toward the doors.

Clara stood up quickly; but Tope spoke to her restrainingly.

"They want us to wait, Miss Jervis," he explained. He pointed out: "You were back there between the acts, and during the second act. The Inspector in charge, Hagan is his name, wants to find out what you saw."

Clara cried: "No!" There was, to Tope's ears, something like hysteria in her tones. "We didn't see anything, don't know anything," she protested. "He has no right . . ."

But Tope urged gently: "You want to help all you can, Miss Jervis. A man dead. That is serious business, for everyone. Nothing to be afraid of, to be panicky, or nervous; but a matter for cool heads, and straight thinking. You'll see that . . ."

But the girl insisted: "I won't. I don't know anything . . ."

Miss Moss spoke crisply. "Clara, be still," she said. And to Inspector Tope: "We will wait, of course." And she asked: "What have they found out? What do they know?"

Tope answered soberly: "Not much, ma'am. This man came to see Miss Cyr. And he's dead in her dressing room. That's all I heard."

"What does she say?" Clint asked sharply; but Tope shook his head.

"She's upset, hasn't been able to talk yet," he replied.

The audience had slipped away; and now ushers moved about the house, turning up seats with sharp, slapping sounds. The cleaning women began to appear. Miss Moss rose.

"We might move into one of the boxes," she suggested. "To be out of their way."

Tope agreed, and he led them through the row of seats to the side aisle, along the aisle to the box nearest. The door that admitted to the stage was just beyond. The lights in the theatre had been dimmed; only enough illumination remained to suffice for the work of house cleaning that now began. The old man saw them all seated, and he was about to return to the stage again, when Hagan appeared in the entrance of the box beside them here.

They swung to look at him, and Inspector Tope, who was not likely to miss any betraying movement, even though he never appeared to be looking in more than one direction at a time, saw Clara's hand press her throat. Then he introduced Hagan to them all, and Hagan said, in an apologetic tone:

"We're waiting for Doc Gero. That's the medical examiner. But I'd like to ask you folks a few questions while we're waiting."

Miss Moss said composedly: "We wish to help in every possible way."

Hagan nodded. "Naturally," he agreed. He spoke to Clint, watching both the young people. "You were back there, all through the second act?"

"Yes, sir," Clint assured him.

"Where did you go when you went back?" Hagan asked; and Clint considered for a moment, and then he said slowly:

"I went to Mat's dressing room. Mat Hews. It's across from Miss Ransom's; and Clara went in with her. When Hews and Miss Ransom went on, we stayed in the wings, watching the show. And after the curtain, we came out here."

Tope wondered whether Hagan would find this brief statement curiously incomplete; but Hagan only nodded twice, as though recording their movements in his memory, and he asked: "You know where Miss Cyr had her dressing room?"

"Yes, sir," Clint assented.

"Could you see it, from where you were?"

"No, you couldn't very well see it unless you were behind the back drop that runs across behind the stage."

"So you didn't see anyone go in or out of her dressing room?"

"No. No sir."

"You see this man that came to call on her? A tall man, in evening clothes, with a soft black hat and a dark overcoat?"

Clint said: "I must have been in Mat's dressing room when he came in."

"You didn't see him?" Hagan insisted.

"No!"

And Clara cried hotly: "He told you he didn't! Why do you ask him again? What do you suppose we know about it? Why do you keep asking us? Mr. Hammond ran away, didn't he? Isn't that enough for you? I won't have you . . ."

Hagan said gravely: "Why, Miss Jervis, it's my job to . . . Hullo, Dunning?"

For while he spoke, Dunning had appeared in the curtained doorway of the box. The officer reported: "Doc Gero's here. Looking at the body now."

Inspector Hagan rose. "Excuse me, folks," he said hurriedly. "I'll be back. You wait here!"

He turned away; and Tope, after a moment's hesitation, looked at Miss Moss. She nodded as though in a command to him; so he followed Hagan through the stage door once more. Hagan said over his shoulder to the older man:

"The girl knows something!"

But he seemed to expect no reply, and Tope made none.

Around Lola Cyr's dressing room, a score of people now were gathered, standing in little groups and clusters, watching that closed door. Hagan opened the door and went in, but Tope stayed outside. He surveyed the folk around him; and then he saw Mat Hews. The older man smiled at the younger; and Mat asked in a low tone:

"Is Clara all right?"

"She's upset," said Tope. "That's all."

The boy frowned ruefully. "Of course," he agreed.

Tope watched him. "But she needn't be," he suggested. "She and her brother were in your dressing room, or Miss Ransom's, all through the intermission. They didn't see anything, didn't see anyone come in. They told Hagan so."

Mat looked at the older man. "They did?" he asked, and his lips were stiff.

"So they're all right," Inspector Tope repeated. "Hagan wants to talk to them a little more, that's all."

Young Mat Hews lighted a cigarette attentively, and he moved away. The Inspector watched him, but he waited here beside the closed door. He had time for thought, and things to think about.

More than once, in these many years of his service, he had acted upon a guess, a hunch, a premonition, an instinctive certainty without factual proof to support it. To use any capacity is to develop it; Tope could read a riddle that might utterly perplex another man. It seemed to him that he read in some measure this whole riddle now. When after a time Hagan came out of the dressing room with Doctor Gero, Tope approached them. He knew the doctor of old; they had worked together many times; they clasped hands now, and Hagan said briefly:

"He was shot. One shot. Thirty-two, Doc says. Close range. And the gun is gone."

He added: "Doc knows him, too."

Inspector Tope looked inquiringly at Gero, and the Medical Examiner nodded.

"I used to know him, that is," he corrected. "He was a doctor here in town; something shady about him; chased women more than he should. A fellow named Canter!"

Tope stood very still; and Doctor Gero reflected: "He was likely to end this way, in some woman's dressing room, with a bullet in him. He was that kind of man!"

Inspector Tope remained a moment more with wagging head, his hands swinging. Then he turned aside, and he said:

"I'll be with Miss Moss and the Jervis children, Hagan. When you want them."

Hagan assented, and Tope moved away.

He found these three in the box where he had left them, Clara still as stone, Clint and Miss Moss talking quietly. Their eyes rose to meet his as he appeared; and the Inspector sat down, and he said briskly:

"Well, things are clearing up. The dead man is a doctor named Canter."

He saw, from the corner of his eye, Clara's shuddering movement; but Miss Moss assented calmly.

"Yes," she agreed. "I thought that must be so!"

6

INSPECTOR Tope had a masterly gift for inactivity. He could strike swift and surely when he chose; but also he could wait, as passive as a turtle on a rock, for days on end. He had built his professional career on the belief that if you give a thief—or a murderer—enough rope, he will hang himself. So tonight he was content to play the part of spectator and nothing more.

Yet though it was true that as he had told Miss Moss he was no longer an officer of the law and bound to its enforcement, this could not prevent his speculations, his shrewd and wise conjectures. And in this particular matter, he had a new and keener interest in watching Miss Moss, in marking how she foresaw each step in the progress of events. An hour ago she had startled him by voicing a question that had only begun to take shape in his own mind. She had asked Clint: "Did Miss Cyr have a caller between the acts; was this man larger than Mr. Hammond?" And now again, when she heard the incredible news that the dead man was that same Doctor Canter who had tended Clarence Peace after his accident two years ago, who had involved Clara Jervis in an ugly scandal, who was presumably in California even now, her only comment was:

"I thought that must be so!"

To Inspector Tope himself the identification of the dead man had come as a complete surprise; so it was the more astonishing to him that Miss Moss showed no surprise at all. And he wondered whether this were because she had facts unknown to him upon which to base her conclusions, or whether it was merely that her instinct was more alert than his. She was a woman, he perceived, whose attainments were not easily to be matched by any man. . . .

"A doctor named Canter, yes," he heard himself saying, in a matter-of-fact tone, as though this name could have no meaning to these others here. "Doctor Gero, the Medical Examiner, knew him. Gave him a bad character."

Miss Moss reflected: "I presume he was shot during the cannonade in the second act, or someone would have heard."

"He was shot, yes," Tope assented. In the dim light here his eyes were screened, but they were attentive too. For he had not told them the manner of this killing.

She seemed to read his thoughts; she said simply: "He was shot, was he not?"

And Tope nodded. "He was," he agreed. "I wondered how you knew."

Miss Moss considered him with a grave attention. "I suppose," she suggested, "that we are all suspects, just now. Yet —you and I were together, Inspector." She smiled faintly. "Need you try to trap me?"

The old man sat with wagging head. He looked at her, and he looked at Clint and Clara here. The girl, he saw, was more composed than she had been a while ago. Clint leaned taut and tender by her side, somehow protectingly; but Clara's head was high, her eyes were steady. And Tope spoke to them and to Miss Moss together, with a sober gravity.

"Why, I'll tell you, ma'am," he proposed. "You're sensible, and so am I. Let's have some calm, sensible talk together."

He leaned forward, his fat hands upon his knees. "Here it is," he said. "I've been in a lot of affairs like this; and there's always someone, and sometimes a lot of people, afraid of getting mixed up in it, or afraid of something else. So they tell part of the truth, or none of the truth. Or sometimes they lie!"

He paused, went on:

"Now, ma'am, there's this about a lie. It can't stand alone. It's got to have other lies to prop it up. You have to be mighty clever, and have a mighty good memory, to make a lie stand up in a thing like this.

"And there's another angle, too. If there's been a killing, and you haven't had any part in that, it don't matter what else you've done. The police want the killer, and they want him quick; and they don't care if you've robbed, or burned, or stole, or what not. So long as you're not in the killing, they're not thinking about you, right at the time."

He hesitated, and these three sat very still. He said at last more gently:

"What I'm trying to tell you all is this. I know, and we all know, that Miss Jervis or her brother here didn't kill this man. Neither one of them. If they had, they'd have acted different. But we all know that they saw this Doctor Canter back there, and maybe talked to him. It's certain they've got something they ought to tell. Only they're afraid. Miss Jervis is afraid of being mixed up somehow in it, and Clint is afraid for her. . . ."

Clint interjected in a slow heat: "Clara's all right! I

won't have her dragged in. Canter had it coming to him. Plenty!"

"He got it—plenty," Tope reminded them. "And that's all right. But you folks made a mistake." His tone was almost pleading. "You told Hagan you didn't see Canter back there. Well, I know you did; and you can be sure there were others saw you looking at him, and maybe talking to him. If you'd been one of the actors, or a stage hand, or something, nobody would have paid any attention to you, or noticed what you did. But you were an outsider, and Miss Jervis too, and Canter; and it's safe to say that someone saw every move you made." He pounded his knee in a sober emphasis. "The thing I'm telling you is, don't lie; don't hide things. Tell Inspector Hagan the truth. Help him all you can. Because the sooner this is cleared up, the better for all of you."

There was a moment's silence; and he watched them, waited.

But Clara said at last: "You don't understand, Inspector." She smiled faintly. "You can't understand, I expect; because you've been a policeman so long. But you see, people are brought up now to be afraid of policemen. Suppose you're driving a car and you see a policeman ahead. You always slow down, just a little, instinctively. Because no one ever knows when he is going to be arrested, summoned to court, fined for some traffic violation. Maybe it didn't used to be so, before automobiles, but we all break laws now. No one drives a car around the block without breaking two or three laws. So we're all criminals, and we're all mistrustful of policemen. They have so much power! If a policeman stops your car and takes you to court for speeding, you haven't a chance, even though all the other cars on the street were going just as fast as you were. You'll be convicted, and fined. . . . It happens to all of us. We all know policemen are tyrannous, and treacherous, when they choose to be, and lenient to some and hard on others; so we're bound to be afraid of them! And when a person is afraid, he will always lie!"

Tope wagged his head. "I know," he agreed. "That's true. A lot of it. It hadn't ought to be so; and it didn't used to be so. I can remember when I was a youngster, if a thing was against the law, you didn't do it. And grown-ups weren't afraid of policemen. But now, most people have either been to court or they've got out of going by knowing someone that could take care of them."

He urged slowly: "But this is murder, Miss. You can trust Inspector Hagan in this. I'm giving you good advice. Honest I am!"

Clara laughed softly, touched his hand. "There!" she whispered. "You're nice! Even if you are a policeman, I'm not afraid of you. . . ."

So Inspector Tope understood that these young people would go their own gait for all his urgencies; and he sighed wearily and said no more. They sat waiting, in the dim-lit auditorium where the cleaning women were finishing their tasks; and by and by a policeman in uniform, young Tim O'Malley, came to fetch them. He appeared in the entrance to the box and spoke to Inspector Tope.

"Hagan wants you folks, Inspector," he explained.

"Hello, Tim," Tope returned. "All right, we'll come along."

Clara, a sudden tremor in her tones, protested: "If he wants to see me, he can come out here!"

But Miss Moss rose briskly, and she collected her belongings; her pocketbook, her glasses, her handkerchief.

"Nonsense, Clara!" she exclaimed. And to O'Malley: "Of course, we'll come, officer!" And to Tope then, as they followed the policeman: "I want to see, to hear. I want to know what happens."

Tope stood aside to let her pass. Clara made some protest still; but Miss Moss was already gone, and Clint took the girl's arm and in some degree compelled her. A moment later they came into the wide emptiness of the stage.

The naked light from that great bulb for a moment blinded them. Tope saw Hagan, and Mat Hews, and Kay, and Max Urbin, and Madison, and some of the stage hands, and the lesser figures in the cast; and these folk all looked toward the little group in silence. Only Mat moved toward them, toward Clara's side.

Hagan waited where he was while they approached him. Miss Moss went directly to him; and Clint and Clara came upon her heels, reluctantly. Tope was behind these two. He remarked the fact that though Mat came loyally to stand by Clara, Kay stayed aloof.

Then Miss Moss spoke to the Inspector.

"You sent for us?" she said.

Inspector Hagan nodded. His eye met that of Tope, and then returned to her again. He did not look at the younger folk. He said slowly:

"Yes, ma'am, I did. I needed you."

"How can I help you?" she asked.

He hesitated. "Well, I'll tell you," he explained.

And then he was silent, for there was a little stir at one side. A policeman opened the door of Miss Cyr's dressing room and two men came out, in the white uniforms of hospital orderlies. They carried between them a stretcher, and upon it, all uncovered, lay a stark, still form.

Tope heard the low, choking whispers all around him; then a pounding silence. In this dreadful silence the two men bore their burden across the stage, and the folk in the way drew hurriedly back to let them pass. Everyone watched them, save that Tope looked at Hagan, and Hagan watched Clara's white countenance, and Miss Moss looked all around, from one face to another, with quick, inquiring eyes.

Then the orderlies were gone, and Clara met Inspector Hagan's glance, and her chin lifted in a steady courage and she smiled.

And Miss Moss prompted him crisply: "You were saying something, Inspector. Before your—experiment!"

He nodded almost sheepishly. "Why, yes," he confessed. "I was telling you how it stands, now."

And he spoke more harshly.

"Here's what we've got," he said. "These two, young Jervis and his sister, came back right after the first act curtain. Miss Ransom was dressing. Miss Jervis went in with her. Hews was dressing, and young Jervis went into his room. Then they all went into Hew's dressing room, and then they all came out, laughing and talking.

"And about that time, Doctor Canter came in. He came up the steps right beside them, and Jervis here saw him, and this young fellow said something to Canter, under his breath.

mad. Someone heard Jervis say: 'I set out to kill you once. I can still do it.' And Canter laughed at him."

He hesitated, watching Clint; he swung suddenly to Clara.

"And then Miss Jervis said something to Canter," he continued. "And Canter grinned and went on, past Hammond's dressing room. Hammond's valet came out and called him back, and Hammond came and spoke to him in the door. Then Canter went on to Miss Cyr's dressing room.

"Nobody saw anything else; and nobody saw Canter again till Miss Cyr found him. As far as we know."

His eyes swung heavily from one of them to another, around the little circle. Clara, Clint, Miss Moss, Tope. Then back to Miss Moss again. He addressed her:

"Now I want these two to tell me what they said to him, and him to them."

Clara cried: "I told you we didn't see him!"

"I know," he assented, almost kindly. "You were scared, lied. That's all right. I don't blame you. Most folks do the same. But you did see him, and talk to him. What did you talk about?"

"I didn't see him," the girl insisted.

Hagan looked at Clint almost appealingly. "I don't want to make trouble for you folks, Jervis," he urged. "Your sister's excited and scared. You tell me what was it all about?"

Clint answered stiffly: "My sister has told you we didn't see him!"

But Miss Moss spoke then; and she smiled. She said: "Be patient with them, Inspector. They are young. I can tell you what happened; what was said."

Inspector Tope saw Clara's eyes widen, saw Clint's movement of incredulous astonishment.

But Miss Moss ignored them, spoke to Hagan. "Clara met Doctor Canter in California," she said explicitly. "He paid her much attention. They went together one afternoon to a roadhouse in the mountains, for dinner; but a snow squall blocked the roads and forced them to stay all night. A woman who was in love with Doctor Canter found them there in the morning and tried to shoot him. The affair got into the papers and resulted in some ugly publicity for Clara.

Clint was in Paris at the time; and he started home to kill Doctor Canter for having compromised his sister. I was able to stop him, to summon Clara home."

She paused a moment, then went on: "So tonight when Clint saw Doctor Canter in the theatre, he warned the man to keep away from Clara; and Doctor Canter said something scornful about Clara. I don't know what, but I suppose she heard him and resented it furiously, and told him so. That is what happened, Inspector, I am sure."

Tope saw that the girl's eyes were brimming. Clara caught the older woman's arm, gripped it tight. "How did you know?" she whispered. "How could you know?"

Miss Moss smiled gently. "I'm an old woman, dear," she returned. "Old women become sometimes very wise!"

And Clara faced Hagan then. "He tried to make love to me that night out there, and I wouldn't let him," she said bravely. "So he called me a poor sport, said I wanted to play with fire without getting burned. And tonight he called Clint a loud-mouthed pup, and he called me a cheat!" Her cheeks were white, but her eyes were steady and fine.

Hagan seemed to consider; and Miss Moss asked: "You see?"

Hagan nodded slowly. "I didn't know about the California end," he admitted. "But I'd have found it out. You saved time by telling me. Now let's go on from there." He turned to Clara.

But before he could put another question, there was an interruption. A woman came toward them across the stage; a woman tall and gaunt, with heavy black hair, and a dark shadow across her upper lip, and deep black eyes. Inspector Hagan turned to meet her; and she said huskily:

"Miss Cyr can see you now!"

Hagan forgot Clara instantly. "Good!" he exclaimed. "I'll come."

But as he turned, Miss Moss touched his arm. "May I come too?" she asked. "Inspector Tope and I? I have some interest here, Inspector. These children have—no one but me."

Hagan hesitated; but Tope urged: "She might help, dealing with this other woman, Hagan. You saw how she guessed that about the young ones. She's quick, wise!"

"I'm not much on handling women," Hagan confessed. "And this one might take handling." He hesitated. "All right, come along," he decided. "We'll see!"

And he led the way across the stage. . . .

Lola Cyr, when she collapsed in the first shock of this tragedy, had been carried into Kay Ransom's dressing room. That way Hagan turned now, and Miss Moss and Inspector Tope followed him, leaving the younger folk behind. Hagan knocked on the door, and someone called:

"Come! Come in, Inspector!"

So Hagan entered, and they followed him. The maid-servant stayed outside.

For a moment after they thus came face to face with Lola Cyr, these three looked at her in that long silence which her appearance always could command. She wore a metal-cloth negligee that fitted her smoothly, leaving her figure's sleek and perfect contours all revealed. Her turban was of the same material, white as silver is white. Her cheeks were warm, her lips a flame, her eyes shadowed pools. Tope, could guess that her beauty was as much art as nature; yet the art was completely effective. This woman half sat, half reclined upon a low couch at one side of the small room, and she looked up at them without any expression in her eyes at all, so that her face was like a mask.

Like a mask of deadly terror, Tope thought; and he was sure of this when after they had stood a minute staring at her thus, she smiled as though her courage were renewed by the fact that she had impressed them so. He understood suddenly that this—for all the bizarre and provocative costume which she wore—was no exotic enchantress; this was a woman, woeful and perturbed, filled with a terror only half concealed.

Inspector Hagan must have seen her across the footlights; yet he asked slowly: "You're Lola Cyr?"

The woman smiled again; "My name is Lily Mount, Inspector. Lola Cyr for the stage, yes. But very much Lily Mount just now."

Hagan cleared his throat in a deep embarrassment. "I expect you're upset," he suggested.

"I was," she assented. "Yes, I suppose I am!"

Tope found himself liking her. Hagan must have felt this too, for he said quickly: "That's all right! I'm trying to find out what happened here; but if you're too tired to talk to me . . ."

"No, I'm rested now."

"Well, I won't bother you any more than I have to," Hagan promised. "This Doctor Canter came to see you?"

She nodded. "Yes," she said.

He asked: "Friend of yours, is he?"

The woman hesitated. "Publicity is meat and drink to us," she explained at last in an ironic tone. "It does an actress no harm to be known as—the pursued of all pursuers. I encouraged him as I encouraged other men. We play a part off the stage, you know, as well as on!"

"Didn't like him?"

She said thoughtfully: "You will hardly understand. I have tried to build a reputation around myself; tried to erect an image in the public mind. Doctor Canter—and other men—were properties, adjuncts of the part I sought to play."

Hagan looked at her doubtfully; and he rubbed his hand across his mouth in a puzzled fashion. He said: "I ought to take that the worst way, ma'am; but somehow it don't sound so, coming from you." He shook his head. "It sounds foolish for me to say so, but I'm betting whatever you did was all right."

She smiled faintly; and Miss Moss moved a little nearer where the other woman sat. Then Hagan said:

"I don't know as I'd feel the same if I were your husband. But I guess you're not married."

She hesitated, and her eyes clouded for a moment; then she said: "Yes. But that doesn't matter now."

Hagan asked in a slow surprise: "Separated, are you?"

"He is not here," she answered.

"Where is he?"

"I don't know."

"Any chance that he came here tonight and killed Canter for chasing after you?"

She shook her head: "He did not kill the doctor. No."

The Inspector hesitated. "Where is he?" he insisted. "What's his name?"

"I do not know where he is," she replied.

So the Inspector turned to the business here in hand. "All right," he commented. "Now Canter came to your dressing room, before the second act."

"Yes."

"Sat down and talked to you?'

"Yes. While I was changing."

"What about when you went on?"

"I left him there."

"Which entrance did you use?"

"The one on this side."

"Who was around that entrance when you went on?"

"I remember a young man, and the usual people in the company."

Inspector Hagan nodded. "A young man and a girl?" he suggested.

"No, this young man was alone," she insisted. "I noticed when he looked at me."

The Inspector glanced at Miss Moss; he urged then: "You might not have noticed the girl. Miss Jervis."

"Clara Jervis?" the woman asked. "Oh, I saw her in California at our rehearsals there. And I've seen her here, but not tonight. I'm sure I would have noticed her."

Hagan stood with bowed head for a moment, returned then to his questioning: "All right. Now you and Hammond were on during the machine gun stuff, weren't you?"

"Yes."

"Young Hews on? Or Miss Ransom?"

"No. The boy goes off just before the guns start; and Miss Ransom is on the staging above, by the elevator shaft, ready to take her cue right after the shooting."

"But you and Hammond were on?"

"Yes."

"Who came off first? You, or him?"

"We came off together," she said, a little wearily. "He went with me to my dressing room."

"Why?" Hagan asked. "Do that often, did he?"

The woman hesitated. "He knew Doctor Canter was there," she confessed. "And he didn't like the man. He was protesting at my receiving the doctor, as we went along behind the back drop to my room."

"And Canter was there?"

She shook her head. "No, when Walter and I got there, he was gone." She explained hurriedly: "Walter Hammond. Mr. Hammond."

Miss Moss watched her attentively, and Lola looked up at the other woman for a moment, as though in faint dismay.

"Canter was gone?" Hagan repeated. "Or you didn't see him, anyway."

"His hat and coat were on the *chaise longue,* but he wasn't there," she assented.

"What did you think?"

"I was a little relieved. I had been afraid he and Mr. Hammond might quarrel. I supposed Doctor Canter had gone out front to watch the act, perhaps; or he might be somewhere back stage."

"Hammond stay there with you?" he asked.

"There's a wardrobe off my dressing room," she explained. "Annette and I went into the wardrobe—it's really a large closet and lavatory combined—and he stayed in the dressing room, talking to me through the open door. Or rather, I was talking to him."

"What about?" he asked.

"I was telling him not to be an idiot about Doctor Canter."

"What did he say?"

She smiled faintly. "Nothing," she said. "He answered me once, and then he didn't answer again; and when I came out—it was only a moment or two—he had gone."

"Gone where?"

"I supposed he'd gone to take his cue. And then Madison came desperately looking for him, said he had disappeared. I didn't know what to think."

"You went on, after that?"

"Yes. And then during the intermission we were all scurrying around. We had to make the third act go. It was a strain, hard on us all."

Hagan hesitated. "And it wasn't till afterwards that you found—him?"

Her lips were white. "After my last exit," she assented. "I was tired, worn out. I went back to my dressing room and sat down and stretched my legs, relaxed. And my foot hit something, under the dressing table. So I leaned over to see what it was."

He said quickly: "Never mind. Don't worry about that."

"His eyes were open!" she whispered. "He was looking up at me!"

"Never mind," he repeated, reassuringly. "I know all about that. Now where do you think Hammond went?"

She said slowly: "I've been trying to guess. I think perhaps he saw Doctor Canter under there. He'd had some trouble, years ago; a scandal that hurt him professionally. I think he was afraid of being involved again, lost his nerve, ran away."

"Any chance Canter could have come back, while you were in the wardrobe?" Hagan asked sharply. "Any chance Hammond could have killed him then?"

"None at all!" she insisted. "I'd have heard the shot, heard any movement. The door was open between, all the time."

Hagan nodded. "Canter was shot while you and Hammond were on the stage, I guess," he agreed. "While the guns were going. If that's so, Hammond didn't do it; but he was a fool to run away!"

"You can't know what it is," she urged, "to be afraid!"

Hagan shook a stubborn head. "Any man that runs away when there's trouble coming is a fool," he insisted. "If you run from a dog, he'll bite you; and if you run from the law, the law will grab you on suspicion. A fool, I say."

And a voice from the doorway echoed: "Yes, so I have decided!"

Lola was on her feet with a single movement; these others swung in quick astonishment to see the man who stood there. It was Walter Hammond himself. He still wore the dead man's hat and coat. His lips were tight, and he was pale and rigid. But he said steadily:

"A fool, yes! So I've come back, Inspector."

Hagan nodded heavily. "Well, that's sensible," he agreed. "Come in, and shut the door!"

7

INSPECTOR HAGAN, and Inspector Tope; Miss Moss, and the woman who called herself Lola Cyr; and now Walter Hammond! These five stood in a compact group in the little dressing room, and they watched one another warily, as though on guard. For a space no one spoke at all.

Then Miss Moss and Inspector Tope, as though there were a bond between them, drew somewhat apart from the others. Tope leaned his shoulders against the wall, and Miss Moss stood precise and erect beside him, her hands clasped in a fashion curiously prim. Lola Cyr, after that first movement which brought her to her feet, seemed to wilt wearily again; she sat down in the chair by the wide dressing table with its frame of lights about the mirror. Hammond looked at her with a long glance, and he moved a little toward her. Then Hagan, wiping his mouth with his hand, crossed to the door as though to bar that egress, and there turned and faced them all.

He said after a moment: "You were wise to come back, Hammond. We'd have had you by morning, anyway."

Hammond nodded: "I suppose so. But I came back because I'm—too tired to run away."

"Tired of what?"

"I had my fill of dodging, years ago," he said ruefully. "Probably you remember. A mess about a woman's dying, after dining with me. The law never even accused me; but the newspapers convicted me. It cost me my job, put me on the street. I went hungry, sometimes. No, I won't dodge any more."

Hagan said, with a certain friendliness in his tones: "I guess you got a bad break; but you're all right in this. Canter was shot; and he must have been shot while the guns were going on the stage, or someone would have heard it. You were on the stage while the guns were going, so that lets you out."

"I know," Hammond agreed. "Thanks."

"So why did you run away?" Hagan asked.

"Scared," the man said.

"Scared of what?"

"When I found him. Scared you'd try to pin it on me!"

There was a long silence, an instant that seemed eternal. Then Hagan coughed; and he repeated: "You found him?"

"Yes."

"When was that?"

So Hammond answered slowly: "Why, when Lola and I made our exit in the second act. I went to her dressing room, stayed to talk to her a minute. She was in the little closet, the wardrobe, with her maid. I sat down on the *chaise longue,* and felt something hard under me, and picked it up. It was a gun!"

The room was taut; but Hagan asked sharply: "Pistol?"

"Revolver. One of these nickel-plated ones. Not a prop. At least I never saw anyone use it in the show. I picked it up, saw it was loaded, with real cartridges. And I broke it, and one of them had been fired. That startled me! I looked around, and the first thing I saw was a man's foot, sticking out from under the curtain around Lola's dressing table."

"All right," Hagan prompted. "Next!"

"Why, I crossed over to see who it was. Thought it might be someone hiding there. . . . And I saw it was Canter, with a spot on his shirt front that told the story."

"So you ran?"

"I shoved his foot out of sight," Hammond assented. "I grabbed his hat and coat off the *chaise longue.* I stuffed the gun under one of the pillows. You'll find it there. And I went out through the door behind the boxes at that end of the stage. There were some folks in the wings, but they were watching the act. No one spotted me."

"Where'd you go?" Hagan asked.

"Walked the streets. Sat in the Common, on a bench. Thought. Came back."

"How'd you get in?"

"The stage door. Peterson told the cop there who I was. The cop told me you were in here." He grinned. "I brushed past him and came in."

Hagan nodded: "That's all right. But when you ducked out, who did you see in the wings?"

"No one. Just the usual people. Urbin. Maybe Hews. I don't know. I slipped by."

Hagan considered. "The trouble with that story is," he said, "the gun wasn't there. Not on the *chaise longue*. Not in the room anywhere. We looked." His eyes turned to meet Lola's. "You didn't find the gun, did you? Didn't see it?"

She shook her head. "Annette may have," she suggested. "Annette was in the dressing room, all the time I was on in the third act. You can ask her."

The Inspector started to open the door, then he hesitated, turned back to them.

"We can come to that," he decided. "I hadn't finished with you, ma'am, before Mr. Hammond came in. We'd come to where you found Doctor Canter, and yelled. Where was this maid of yours then?"

"Right there, with me. Rubbing my temples, my head . . ."

"What happened? I mean, you leaned over, and saw him, and yelled. Then what?"

Lola smiled faintly. "It was funny," she confessed. "In a way." And she explained: "You see, my hair is not my crowning glory. So for the public, I always wear a turban, or an obvious wig, or something. Annette had taken off my turban to rub my head; and when I screamed, she knew someone would come in very quickly. So she fairly grappled me, and dragged the turban down on my head again. And I fought her, frantic, hysterical . . . I can see that it was funny now!"

"But someone did come in?"

"Mat Hews," she agreed. "And Kay Ransom. They'd been standing in the wings at that end of the stage, watching the final scene, watching poor Madison fumble through his lines in Mr. Hammond's place. They came in; and I remember Kay helped Annette quiet me. I was having some mild hysterics, in a curiously detached way. I was perfectly calm, like a spectator, watching myself sob and writhe and moan. They laid me on the floor, and I remember kicking my heels to hear them clatter. Then I watched Mat Hews, and he was so busy that I forgot to kick, after a while."

"Busy? Doing what?"

"Down on his knees staring at Doctor Canter! And then rummaging around the room! He had a handkerchief in his hand. I used to have a cocker spaniel. I'd hide my handkerchief and he'd go nosing everywhere till he found it. Mat reminded me of the little dog, with that handkerchief in his hand, and I started to laugh, and Kay and Annette thought I was worse, and then someone else came in. A lot of people."

"How long was this?" Hagan asked. "After you yelled."

"I don't think it was long," she confessed. "You know how time stands still sometimes and you remember a scene as though it were a picture. It couldn't have been long. Then Kay and Annette helped me over here to Kay's dressing room; and then Annette put Kay out, and took care of me."

"You've been here since?"

"Ever since."

The Inspector sighed and wiped his mouth with his hand. "Well," he said, half to himself, "that finishes with you, anyway." He looked toward Inspector Tope. "I'd say it wasn't her, and it wasn't Hammond," he suggested.

Tope nodded; but Miss Moss spoke quietly. "And it wasn't Alexander the Great; nor General Grant," she remarked in mild irony.

Hagan frowned, shook his head. "You don't think I'm getting anywhere," he protested. "But the first thing is to find out what happened, how it happened, all about it." He continued: "You see here, now. We're getting somewhere. The gun was there, when Hammond saw it. All right, what does that show? It shows that whoever shot Canter didn't have time to get away right off. So he dropped the gun there, and when Miss Cyr yelled and the crowd pushed in, whoever killed Canter went in too, and picked up the gun and got away with it.

"All right, why did he do that? Why, because someone would know it was his gun! If it wasn't, he wouldn't care. He'd let it be found. So all we've got to do is find that gun.

It's here somewhere. We'll find it, and trace it by the number, and clean up the whole thing!"

Miss Moss returned: "I see!" Her voice was to Hagan's ears toneless; but Inspector Tope was not so deaf as he. The older man's eyes twinkled faintly. Hagan was a good man, and a thorough man, and he asked the right questions, and he got the facts. If he seemed stupid, that might be a part of his strength. Let him go on, grope his own way to the light. It was the man's right so to do.

Yet—there were some things Tope knew which Hagan did not know; and the older man now moved to put these facts into Hagan's hands. He said to the other:

"Hagan, you remember I told you a while ago about Dave Howell, and this man Peace?" Hagan looked at him in some bewilderment, then made a sign of assent. And Tope turned to Walter Hammond.

"You knew Clarence Peace, didn't you, Mr. Hammond?" he asked.

Hammond said readily: "Yes. Yes, I knew him."

"You knew he'd disappeared?"

"I knew he'd not been around for a while back, a month or so."

Tope urged: "Didn't Inspector Howell come here and ask you some questions about him? Didn't Peace come here to see you one night, and drop out of sight?"

Hammond hesitated; his tone was mildly impatient: "Yes. Inspector Howell asked me some questions, and I answered them. I didn't know what it was all about. Clarence's affairs were his own business, so far as I was concerned."

But Tope suggested: "Tell us about it now. About that time Peace came here."

Hammond considered. "Why, it was several weeks ago," he explained. "But as I recall it, he dropped in during the second act. I spoke to him a minute in the wings. He said he was going to Washington that night. I'm on, most of the second act; so he said he'd wait in my dressing room. When I came off at the curtain, he was gone. I didn't think any more about it till Inspector Howell came to see me, two or three days later."

Hagan asked Tope impatiently: "What's the idea, Inspector? What's that got to do with this?"

But before Tope could reply, Hammond volunteered: "There was one other thing . . . I've thought since that Howell might want to know about it. Peace had a flask, and he gave my man a drink and it made the man dizzy. He went outside, into the passage by the stage door for some air. I had to send for him when I came off!"

"That left Peace alone in your dressing room?" Tope asked quickly.

"Yes. I didn't think to tell Howell; and I fired Lesser—that was my man's name—a day or two later. He had been drinking too much, right along. So I don't think Howell ever talked to him."

"Where is he now? This Lesser?"

"I've no notion," Hammond declared.

Tope said with a mild smile: "I've always figured I'd like to have a valet myself. If I could have a wish, that's what I'd wish for."

They all chuckled; and Hammond explained defensively: "A valet's a necessity, for an actor. So many changes, so many properties to watch, and all that."

But Hagan protested: "Tope, this is off the track. You're wasting time."

"Maybe," Tope agreed. "But I thought it might mean something. Because, you see, Hammond knew Peace, and Peace and Doctor Canter were friends."

Hagan considered. "What of it?" he asked then.

"It just struck me," Tope confessed. "A coincidence, in a way. Peace steals four hundred thousand and disappears; and now Canter's dead. . . ."

Hagan scratched his head. "I don't see any way that could fit in here," he insisted. He looked at Hammond doubtfully. "You knew Doctor Canter, did you?"

"I knew him years ago," Hammond assented. "Met him again in California last winter. And then he followed us East; or he came East and looked us up."

Hagan suggested shrewdly. "Looked Miss Cyr up, you mean, don't you?" He saw Hammond's red confusion, and he exclaimed: "That reminds me! She said you were sore at him for hanging around her. Why was that? Crazy about her yourself, are you? What was it to you?"

Hammond did not immediately answer; he looked at Lola doubtfully. But Miss Moss spoke.

"It was very natural," she said quietly. "You see, Miss Cyr is really Mrs. Hammond."

And they all swung toward her in startled surprise.

"Who told you?" Hagan demanded; and Miss Moss answered, speaking to Lola and not to him:

"You did, Mrs. Hammond. When you used his first name by mistake, then tried to correct your slip!"

Hagan stood bewildered and uncertain, and Hammond said grudgingly: "It's so. We didn't talk about it. Kept it secret. But we've been married seven years!"

"I've a boy five years old," said Lola to Miss Moss, as though appealingly. "He's in school, in Chicago!"

Hagan rubbed his head in a deep exasperation. "There's too much going on here for me," he confessed. "But I know we're off the track, anyway. The thing we've got to do is find that gun." And he asked Lola: "Where's that woman, your maid?"

"Outside the door," Lola guessed; and Hagan went to see. Annette was there, attentive, waiting; he signed to her to come in.

The French woman faced them steadily, and Lola said to her, in low-toned command: "We are telling the truth, Annette."

"You'd better," Hagan agreed. His own bewilderment could turn to anger. He asked the maid: "You stayed in the dressing room from the time Mr. Hammond was there till you found Doctor Canter?"

"Yes," the woman answered.

"There was a pistol, a revolver, under the cushions on the *chaise longue*," said Hagan. "Did you see it?"

"No."

"Did you clean up, straighten the cushions or anything?"

"No."

"Did anybody come in there?"

"No one came in."

Hagan caught the reservation in her tones. "Anyone come to the door?"

"A young man, Mr. Jervis," said Annette; and these others looked at her in intent surprise.

"What did he want?" Hagan barked.

"Just after Miss Cyr went on again, while they were hunting for Mr. Hammond, he came to the door."

"Hunting Hammond, was he?" Hagan demanded.

"He was hunting for his sister."

"His sister?" Hagan's tone was one of stark surprise.

"Yes."

"What made him think she might be in there?"

"I don't know."

"You hadn't seen her?"

"No."

Hagan considered. "See here," he asked, "before that, when Miss Cyr was on, and during the shooting, where were you?"

"In the basement."

"The basement? What for?"

"I hate noise, hate guns."

"You do, eh?"

"I am a French woman," said Annette. "Before the war, I was in this country; but when the war came I went home to nurse. I was in a hospital, and we were bombarded, and there was fighting near."

"Oh," Hagan muttered. "Sorry, ma'am."

"So every night, when I know there will be guns, I go as far away as I can."

And Hagan seemed to see this tall gaunt woman with new eyes. "I'm sorry, ma'am," he said again, and he added reassuringly: "I don't like guns myself."

But Lola told them, mischievously: "Besides, Annette has a swain. When she was most fearful, he would always comfort her. When a woman is afraid, men like to reassure her; so sometimes she may pretend more terror than she feels, to give them opportunity."

Annette said in a grim amusement: "Oh, that one!" It was plain this was a stale jest between them. She looked again toward Inspector Hagan, waiting; and after a moment Hagan cleared his throat, spoke to Miss Moss.

"The way it looks to me, ma'am," he confessed uncomfortably, "I'd better talk to young Jervis about this, now."

Miss Moss agreed. "Yes," she said. "Yes, it is necessary!"

So Hagan opened the door again; he signed to Annette to go before him; he followed her, closed the door behind him, and after a moment he returned with Clint upon his heels. The young man met their glances, and Miss Moss asked:

"Where's Clara, Clint?"

"With Mat," he explained. "She's all right."

Miss Moss spoke to Hagan. "Let me," she suggested; and the Inspector after a moment nodded. So she said to the young man:

"Clint, you and Clara have hidden something. You were not together all the time back stage here tonight. Tell us about that, please."

Clint's color rose and faded. His eye turned from one to the other; and he said stubbornly: "Clara's all right!"

"I've known Clara since she was a baby," Miss Moss reminded him with some asperity. "And you, too. You need not reassure me. Tell us what happened, Clint."

He hesitated. "We'd had a kind of a row," he confessed. "She was sore at me!"

"About Doctor Canter?"

"No." He spoke with a sudden haste. "Well, here's what happened," he said abruptly. "If you've got to know. When Mat and Kay went on, we stood in the wings to watch them. Then Kay went off. Clara said she was going to find Kay, and she went around behind the back drop."

Miss Moss interrupted, voicing the thought that leaped to all their minds. "That would take her past the door of Miss Cyr's dressing room?"

"Yes," he admitted. "She started away, and I told her to keep away from Doctor Canter; and she didn't answer. I stayed there; and then after the shooting on the stage, when Hammond and Miss Cyr came off, I looked around for Clara and she hadn't come back. So I started to hunt for her."

"Did you find her?"

"Yes. Over in the wings on the other side, watching the excitement on the stage. That was after Hammond had gone, you understand."

"Where had she been?" Miss Moss insisted.

"I didn't ask her."

The woman hesitated; she asked at last: "Where did you look?"

"Oh, around!"

"In Miss Cyr's dressing room?"

"No. Of course not. Why should I?"

Her voice suddenly was stern. "Clint, this is no time for lies. Why did you go to Miss Cyr's dressing room to look for Clara? Why did you think she might be there?"

Clint's face was crimson; he licked his lips. He said angrily at last: "She'd made a fool of herself over Doctor Canter before, and she might again. She knew he was there!"

"You thought she might have gone to talk to him?"

"Yes. And he had disappeared too. Nobody missed him but me; but I thought they might be in there together, or somewhere."

Miss Moss nodded. "And that's all?"

"Sure," he said, and wiped his brow.

Inspector Tope moved slightly; but then he checked himself again with a quick satisfaction. For Miss Moss had asked the questions he himself had been about to put to this young man. She remarked:

"You and Clara had had a quarrel. What about, Clint?"

"Oh, this Canter business."

"What about, Clint?" she insisted.

He stood trembling. He said at last miserably: "Why, when we were all in Mat's dressing room, she saw a gun in his drawer and picked it up. She was fooling with it, and I told her to be careful; told her it might be loaded. She said I was silly; and then Mat saw she had the gun, and tried to take it away from her. And she was kidding, and she backed out into the hall away from him. That was when Doctor Canter was just coming in."

There was a deep silence here; but Miss Moss asked bravely:

"She still had this gun in her hands, when you first saw Doctor Canter?"

"Yes."

"What did she do with it?"

"I don't know. I didn't notice, forgot about it."

"What kind of a gun?" the woman persisted; and he said desperately:

"Miss Moss, you don't think Clara had anything to do . . ."

"What kind of a gun, Clint?" she repeated monotonously.

"Oh, a cheap little nickel-plated thing. . . ."

Hagan stepped swiftly toward the door, he opened it and called: "O'Malley!" There was a movement outside, and a voice, and Hagan asked: "Where's Miss Jervis?"

"With young Hews," O'Malley reported. "In his dressing room."

"Fetch 'em here," said Hagan crisply.

And he stood in the open door, turning to face these folk within the room while he waited.

But a moment later O'Malley returned. They all could hear his quick, excited tones.

"They're gone!" he reported. "Out the window into the alley."

"Both of them?"

"Sure."

Hagan's face was red with rage. He whirled on the folk here within the room. "They've taken it on the run!" he cried in furious accusation. "While you kept me jawing here!" And over his shoulder to O'Malley: "Get Headquarters on the phone!"

Inspector Hagan, when he heard that Mat and Clara had vanished, turned on Miss Moss and these others here like an exasperated bear; but only for a moment. Then he made haste to spread the alarm, to seek to close every avenue of escape from the city. There was a telephone in the corridor just outside the dressing room, and they could hear the man's excited, furious words. They did not speak; they simply waited. But Inspector Tope and Miss Moss looked at one another, consulting silently, considering how to meet this situation which did confront them now.

Then Hagan came stumping back into the room and he spoke to Tope in a restrained wrath. "You're to blame for this!" he exclaimed. "I had a hunch it was the girl, all the time. If they hadn't been friends of yours . . ."

Miss Moss protested: "You assume a great deal, do you not?"

But it was Tope who answered her. "Why, ma'am, the Inspector here, he's right to blame me," he said.

"At least, whatever Clara has done, you're not to blame," she insisted loyally.

Inspector Tope hesitated, and he wagged his head. "Why, yes," he said at last. "Yes, I guess I am."

"You couldn't know these two would—run away!"

And Tope insisted equably: "Yes, ma'am, I thought they would. I as good as told them to," he said.

Hagan stared at him with lowered brows. He shook his head as though to clear his vision. "I figured you'd be on my side," he said morosely. "I ought to run you in, old man. Accessory after the fact . . ."

Tope interposed. "You talk too much, Inspector," he objected, in a wholly respectful tone. "You talk too much, and you don't think enough. You know everything I know, as far as facts go; so there's no accessory business about this. The trouble with you is, you're thinking about who killed Doctor Canter, and you can't see anything else."

"What else is there to see?" Hagan protested; and these others here listened with a grave attention. Young Clint was near the door, watching them all, twitching at his lip with his finger. Miss Moss was attentive and composed; only now and then she rubbed the back of one gloved hand with the palm of the other, as though smoothing the nap upon the suede. Hammond had come to Lola's side, stood by her there as though protectingly. Her glowing beauty was like a radiance in the room. And:

"What else is there to see?" Hagan cried.

"So much!" Tope exclaimed. "A thousand things! Man, when there's a murder, the world doesn't stop moving. There are always a lot of things, little happenings, running down the chutes of time, like a wheat elevator. And a murder is just one of them, like a lump of coal in the wheat. You may miss seeing the lump of coal; but if you look over all the grains of wheat, you'll find some that are smutted up with coal dust, and some that are bruised and scratched by the lump, and so on."

He hesitated, smiled, said like a dreaming old man:

"Why, in the old days, when I had your job, I never spent much time trying to find out what folks did before the killing, or while it was going on. I was always watching to see what they'd do afterwards. Throw a rock in water, and the waves keep rippling for a long time. I remember once there was a shooting, and no telling who did it. One of the men that knew the dead man moved away, two years after. I kept track of him, and I used to look him up, once in a while. One day a door slammed in the wind, right behind him, and he jumped; and he turned pale and sweated too. Anybody might jump at a sudden noise like that; but he turned white besides. So I arrested him, and it was him."

Hagan insisted harshly: "If this girl hadn't been a friend of yours, I'd . . ."

But Tope urged: "Don't be too quick at arresting people, Hagan. A policeman only has two kinds of people that he ought to arrest. One is the kind he's sure are guilty; because they deserve it. And the other is the kind he's sure are innocent and sure they can prove it, because it won't hurt them, and it may make the guilty man careless if someone else is arrested. You don't know about Miss Jervis, one way or the other. Till you do, let her alone."

But Hagan said grimly: "Watch me!" He looked at Clint and Miss Moss for a moment. "You two," he directed. "You go home! I'll know where to look for you."

Clint moved as though in relief; but Miss Moss demurred. "I'd like to make one suggestion, if you please," she remarked.

"What's that?"

"There was an actor," said the woman steadily. "On the stage with young Mr. Hews. One of the principals. He was the other gangster . . ."

Hammond suggested: "Max Urbin?"

"If you'll send for him," Miss Moss proposed, "I'd like to ask him a question or two."

Hagan hesitated; but there was something in this woman which compelled respect and even obedience. So a moment later Urbin appeared in the door of this small room. He was, in this light, an old man; one of those good troupers who have trod the boards for years, and never had a big part, and never had a small one. One of those old adepts of the stage who can do any bit of business and do it well. He faced them gravely now; and Hammond said reassuringly:

"Hello, Max."

Urbin nodded: "You back, Walter? Man, you gave Madison a job to do tonight!"

"Sorry," Hammond said; and Hagan interrupted impatiently:

"Urbin, this lady's got something she wants to ask you. . . ."

The old actor bowed to Miss Moss; his smile was amiable. And she said precisely: "Just this, Mr. Urbin. You and Mr. Hews made your exit together, in the second act."

"Yes."

"You stepped into the elevator, out of sight. Did you stay there while the machine guns were going?"

Urban shook his head. "They shoot dummy bullets in those guns, madam," he explained. "Paper wads. They would hurt a man if they hit him; so when we go off, we step out of the way before the shooting starts."

"Did you do that tonight?"

"Yes."

"Was Mr. Hews with you?"

"Yes."

"And you did not come on again? Your part in the performance was done?"

"Why, yes," he said. "None of us appear again except Mat. He lies down in the elevator, after the fusillade, so Miss Ransom can be appropriately grief-stricken over his supposed corpse. And then of course it turns out that he's only wounded, and he recovers later on."

"But it is some time," she suggested, "between his exit and his reappearance in this passive rôle."

He reflected: "It is only about half a minute, I should think."

"What did you and he do during that half minute tonight?" Miss Moss asked; and Urbin chuckled.

"I lit a cigarette," he confessed, with a grin at Inspector Hagan. "Fire laws don't always hold, back stage, you know, Inspector. And Mat took a drag, too; and by that time, the shooting was over and it was time for him to lie down and play dead."

"So he was with you?"

"Yes."

Miss Moss looked at Inspector Hagan. "Then it wasn't he," she pointed out.

But Hagan cried: "I never said he did it! It's the girl . . ."

Miss Moss smiled. "You're absurd!" she told him. "I'm quite sure about Clara; and now of course I'm equally sure about him!"

"Just the same," said Hagan, "I'll be glad to see them bring her in." He stood baffled for a moment; he said then: "Where do you live? Where does she live? Let's have your addresses."

Miss Moss quietly gave him the street and number; he set them down. "All right," he repeated then. "Go home, and stay around till I want you; and if you hear from the girl, tell her she'll save trouble by turning herself in."

"I'll tell her nothing of the kind," Miss Moss retorted; and his face was black with wrath, but he only shook his head.

"Suit yourself," he muttered. "Anyway, get out of here!"

So Inspector Tope and Miss Moss and Clint turned to go. When they all emerged from the dressing room into the corridor, Madison, the stage manager, buttonholed the Inspector. The man was frowning with his own importance.

"I thought you'd want this, Inspector," he suggested. "Here's a list of the cast, and the stage hands, and electricians. Everyone who was back stage. And Inspector, there are reporters out front. Luther—he's our press agent—is there with them, but they want to see you."

Hagan took the sheets of paper Madison handed him, and looked at them and scratched his head. "Well, we'll have to check them all," he confessed. "But it's the Jervis girl, I guess!"

"Miss Jervis?" Madison exclaimed in astonishment. Tope

saw Kay Ransom listening a little to one side; saw the quick turn of her head. Then he himself spoke to Madison.

"No," he told the man. "Inspector Hagan didn't mean that. He wants to see Miss Jervis, that's all."

And Hagan lamely confirmed this. "That's right. I just want to talk to her," he declared.

Then Clint touched Hagan's elbow. "Inspector, may Miss Ransom go with us now?" he suggested. "Kay, I'll see you home."

Hagan looked at the girl appraisingly; but before he could speak Kay said: "Heavens, I'm not ready to go yet, with all this excitement! Besides, the Inspector hasn't cross-examined me!"

Clint protested: "You don't know anything about this."

But she retorted: "Is that so, my dear? Well, let me tell you, when I get a chance to make the headlines . . . 'Beautiful Ingenue Gives Clew to Murder!' I refuse to go until I've told him everything!" She drawled the last word impressively.

Hagan stared at her, and Clint drew her angrily aside; and then Hammond asked: "What about Miss Cyr and myself, Inspector?"

Hagan indifferently nodded, still watching Kay yonder. "You can go, too," he said. "Where do you live?" But when Hammond gave him the address, his interest quickened. "Hello!" he exclaimed, and he looked at Miss Moss. "You're both the same!"

"It's an apartment building," Hammond explained. "I've lodged there during the run of the show."

Hagan considered this for a moment wearily. "All right," he said then. "You can go along." And he asked Madison: "Where are the reporters?"

"Out front."

"You folks dodge them," Hagan directed. "Keep your mouths shut. Any talking to be done, I'll do it. Go out the back way."

Lola suggested: "I must dress. My clothes are in my dressing room."

The Inspector shook his head. "You can put on a coat over what you've got on," he decided. "One of my men will fetch it. I don't want that room touched yet, till I can give it a going over. Finger prints, maybe."

Miss Moss said smilingly: "You won't find any finger prints, I'm afraid."

"Why not?" he asked truculently; and she told him:

"Because young Mat Hews wiped them all off with his handkerchief. At the same time he took the gun!"

She delivered this bomb shell in a tone completely matter of fact; but it left Hagan speechless. Then with no other words she turned and walked away from him. Inspector Tope chuckled, and he drew up beside her. Hagan stared after them; he made one step to follow. Then he shook his head hopelessly and turned away.

Clint overtook them at the stage door—alone; and to Inspector Tope's inquiring glance he said miserably:

"She isn't coming!"

Tope asked gravely: "Can she tell him anything he doesn't know?"

"I don't see how," Clint insisted. "If she can, I don't know what it is." And he added in a sick regret: "I sort of liked Kay."

Miss Moss slipped her arm through his, reassuringly. "Don't be too hard on her, Clint," she suggested. "She is very young." He nodded, and her eyes met those of Inspector Tope. She saw the surprise in his countenance. He had thought she did not like Kay, was surprised that she should defend the girl now. She read his thoughts and smiled at his masculine blindness. Then they said good night to Peterson at the stage door and stepped into the narrow passage outside. A flashlight flared in their very faces; and when their eyes recovered from the glare, Tope saw a group of half a dozen men here confronting them.

He spoke in an amused and friendly tone. "Hello, boys," he said. "We had orders to keep away from you! Thought you were out front!"

Young Charlie Harquail was here. He exclaimed: "You, Tope? Have they called you in?"

"I was in the audience," Inspector Tope explained. "Miss Moss, this is Charlie Harquail, an old friend of mine. He's on the *Journal*. And these other gentlemen. Hello, Dankert. Hello, Gail. And this is Clint Jervis, gentlemen."

Charlie Harquail was the spokesman for them all. "What's the dope, Inspector?" he asked. "What have they got?"

"What have you got?" Tope countered.

"Why, we know the dead man is Doctor Canter; know he was killed in Miss Cyr's dressing room. How does it look to you, Inspector? Any line?"

Inspector Tope wagged his head. "Why, boys," he said, "I'm retired. It's not my business, now. Hagan's on the job; you'll have to talk to him."

"What do you think?" Charlie urged.

Tope protested: "Now, Charlie, you know I never was a hand to say what I think. I only say a thing when I know it. But I'll tell you what Hagan thinks, if that's any good to you." He looked toward Miss Moss in the shadows there for her dissent, but she made no sign; so he said calmly: "Hagan thinks Miss Jervis shot Canter. Clara Jervis. This young fellow is her brother. Miss Moss here is a sort of guardian . . ."

"A girl?" Charlie cried eagerly. "Where is she?"

"She and young Hews—you remember him, in the show, Charlie—they've gone," said Tope.

"Run away?"

"Well, they may not have run," the old man said, in a droll tone. "But that's Hagan's idea! Anyway, they're gone."

The reporters stared uncertainly; he was so completely casual and unconcerned. Then Charlie Harquail asked Miss Moss: "Is that so? What do you say about it?"

Miss Moss said smilingly: "I enjoyed watching Inspector Hagan's mental processes. He seems a most determined man."

And Tope told her with a chuckle: "The boys all know Hagan! The Inspector works hard, and he does the best he can. Good night, son. Good night, boys."

So he left them laughing at his words. He had dismissed Hagan's theories with such a friendly, sympathetic smile. Tope called a taxicab and he and Miss Moss and Clint got in and drove away.

But then Clint leaned toward the old man, half-puzzled,

half-angry. "What did you tell them for, Inspector?" he protested. "Now there'll be another splash in the papers; another dirty scandal."

Tope looked at Miss Moss, smilingly; and she explained to Clint.

"They'd have found out about Clara and Mat anyway," she pointed out. "But if they got it from Hagan, or dug it up themselves, they'd take it seriously. As long as they saw that Inspector Tope and I laughed at it, they'll go easy on Clara; maybe laugh at Hagan a little bit themselves."

And Tope added wisely: "I've had a lot to do with newspaper men in my time, son. I always found it paid to tell them things—if they were bound to find out anyway."

Clint nodded his doubtful understanding; and for a while they rode in silence. Then the young man confessed unhappily: "Just the same, I'd like to know where Clara was tonight, during that second act, after she left me."

Miss Moss said gravely: "I feel sure she spoke to Doctor Canter!" And at Clint's ejaculation she explained: "Clara is headstrong, with a hot, reckless temper. She would pass the door of Miss Cyr's dressing room, in going across the back of the stage. If the door were open, she might see him; and if she did, she would surely go in. How long was it, Clint, that she was gone?"

"Five minutes, maybe ten," he said. "I don't think she left me till after Hammond and Miss Cyr went on. After that there's a scene between Hammond and Urbin; and then the guns; and then the police; and then Hammond and Miss Cyr come off. When it was time for Hammond's next entrance—it wasn't long—they missed him; and it was after that I started to hunt for Clara."

For a while then they said no more. The hour was late, the streets deserted, the night was chill and cold. Inspector Tope looked once or twice at the woman by his side. Seated here, somehow relaxed, she wore no longer that aspect of assurance and composure which was her habit; rather she was suddenly small, and soft and fragile, and he said awkwardly:

"I wouldn't be surprised if you're pretty tired. So much going on; so late and all."

She shook her head. "No, I don't think so," she assured

him. "I don't feel tired. Perhaps I am, without knowing it. I'm trying to think this out."

He nodded soberly. "A thing like this takes hold of you," he assented. "You dream it at night and think it all day, and there's nothing but confusion in it, till all of a sudden it falls into line, all clear."

"I shall want to talk with you tomorrow," she suggested. "To talk it over, from the beginning." And she added after a moment: "Something you said tonight; you said you told Mat to take Clara away. Was that true?"

The old man chuckled. "Mat couldn't swear to it," he assured her. "But—I'd watched them. A blind man could see how it is with them."

"Yes," she agreed.

"When we came back stage," Tope explained, "I told him that she'd lied to Hagan. That is, I told him what she said. Hews would know it was a lie; and he'd know she'd get in trouble by it. I thought he'd do something about it if he could; maybe get her away and give her a chance to calm down."

"They'll be back, of course," Miss Moss murmured.

"Certain," he assented.

"But I wish I knew," she reflected, half to herself. "I've never had a daughter of my own, of course. But Clara's been —like one, in my heart, always."

Tope said reassuringly: "Oh, she'll be fine!"

So they came home, and alighted all together, and paused for a moment between the curb and the door of the lobby; and Tope remarked: "A raw, ugly night."

"Yes." She stood thoughtfully.

Clint, with an instinctive courtesy, moved away from them, waited by the door; and Tope asked Miss Moss: "Anything worrying you? Anything I can do?"

She hesitated, said at last in a slow passion: "I feel that this is—our concern, Inspector. That we ought to help. We must find the truth, somehow!" She whispered, shaken: "It hits so close home to me."

"It will straighten out," he promised.

"I want to have a hand in it," she insisted. "But Inspector Hagan is—hostile. He doesn't accept suggestions."

"That's so," Tope agreed. "Hagan doesn't want any—helping. But ma'am," he suggested, "we can take a hand. I'll get hold of Dave Howell. He'll want to check up on this business tonight; see if he can hook it up with Peace, anyway. We can work through Dave."

Her head lifted in a quick attention, but before she could speak, another taxicab stopped beside them, and Hammond and Lola Cyr alighted. Tope could see the silver gleam of the woman's turban; the warmth of her beauty for a moment filled the night about them. Hammond paid off the cab, and these two looked at Tope and Miss Moss for a moment, hesitantly. Then Hammond touched Lola's arm and with only a nod of greeting they crossed the sidewalk, passed Clint, went inside.

Tope said: "I thought they were going to speak to us."

Miss Moss nodded. "Yes," she agreed, and she added quietly: "The woman is afraid."

And then, in a decisive tone: "Inspector Tope, you spoke of Howell. His particular province is—financial matters, isn't it? He must know people in banks, and business men, and brokers."

"He does," he told her. "Yes, ma'am."

"Go to him," she directed. "Do this for me. Have him find out as much as he can about Doctor Canter. His business affairs, whether he has suffered or prospered, his income tax returns, how much money he has had, and spent, these last two years."

Tope looked at her appreciatively. "Now I hadn't thought of that," he admitted. "Ma'am, you're miles ahead of me. You mean, ever since he took care of Peace, after Peace's accident?"

"Yes."

"I will," he assented. "I'll see Dave, and tell you what he says, tomorrow."

She smiled her thanks, extended her hand.

He took it, and for a moment he held it firmly; and there was some word he wished to say. The word came stammering to his lips, but it died there. He released her hand and she moved away. Clint called good night to him.

When they were gone indoors, Tope took off his hat and

wiped his brow; and he grinned, standing there alone. He had always a keen sense of the absurd. Certainly it was absurd enough that at his age, at three o'clock of a raw cold winter morning, on the sidewalk of an empty street, he should wish to tell a woman that he liked her.

Still grinning, he began to walk back toward town. He might have ridden; for it was cold. But he was warm and content and comfortable. The good world pleased the man, just now.

8

INSPECTOR TOPE opened his eyes next morning, in that comfortable room on Boylston Street which was his home, deeply at peace; and not till full awakening banished that dreamy half-sleep which at first possessed the man, did he realize the incongruity of his present mood. Yet there was, he reminded himself then, little enough reason for contentment, or for peace. Here was a murder done; a murder which came close home to these folk who were suddenly so important in his eyes. Here was a murder done, and a fortune stolen; and yet he was content and at his ease! He sat up in bed with a shake of the head at his own folly. Murders grow cold, and thieving too! If anything were to be accomplished in this matter, it had best be quickly.

He found the morning papers as usual in a heap outside his door; and he brought them in and during the next half hour, while he went about the business of preparing for the day, he read them with sidelong glances over the blade of his razor, or while he whipped a towel about his shoulders, or while he tugged at his socks and laced his shoes. By the time he was dressed, he had absorbed all that they had to say about the affair of the night before.

He saw that his frankness in the matter of Clara's flight with young Mat Hews had had its results. Charlie Harquail had written:

Romance entered into the case late last night when it was learned that among the visitors back stage during the performance was Miss

Clara Jervis, daughter of the late Dana Jervis. She and her brother Clinton spent the intermission before the second act in the dressing room of Mat Hews, juvenile star of the show.

Mr. Hews and Miss Jervis met while they were both students in a dramatic school in California; and when the company came east to open in Boston, Miss Jervis gave up her own dramatic career and returned to her home here.

Neither Mr. Hews nor Miss Jervis could be found last night. It is thought possible that they may be able to throw some light on the tragic happenings which took place behind the scenes during the second act.

Tope found that the other morning papers had been equally cautious, avoiding any least suggestion that either Clara or Mat had more than an accidental connection with the murder. Two of them did print Clara's photograph, obtained from some photographer; but this was to be expected and he was not surprised.

The bulk of the stories, inevitably, centered around the picturesque figure of Lola Cyr, in whose dressing room the dead man's body had been found; the legend which she had erected about herself was strengthened now. She was a modern Lorelei, the siren whose charms attracted Doctor Canter to the spot where he met his death; and none of the reporters failed to remark upon this fact. Her most alluring photographs were included in the layouts published to illustrate the stories; and Tope, reading, paused for a moment to remember the woman as he had seen her the night before, radiant with a lustrous beauty despite the fears she fought always to control.

By the time he had dressed, he found himself hungry for breakfast. This was not usual with the old man; but he had no scruples about satisfying his appetite. He had been a pudgy, round figure for forty years and he was content with his own girth. But before he went downstairs he telephoned Dave Howell; he caught the Inspector at Headquarters, and Tope said earnestly:

"Dave, have you got anything on Peace, since yesterday?"

"Not a thing," Dave confessed. "Not a line."

"I've got an idea," Tope told him. "I want to see you. I'm going down to breakfast now." He named the restaurant. "Can you meet me there, right away?"

"What's up?" Howell objected doubtfully. "I've got a lot to do."

Tope hesitated; he said then: "You saw this Canter thing?"

"Yes."

"Well, Canter is the doctor who fixed Peace up after he was supposed to be hurt, two years ago."

There was a long silence; then Howell asked: "What of it?"

"Come up here," Tope insisted. "And I'll show you."

And when Howell had agreed to come, Tope descended, and strolled along Boylston Street to the restaurant where the other man would meet him. He had not much more than ordered his orange juice and poached eggs before Howell appeared, saw Tope at his table, and came striding across the floor. Dave was always an impatient man; and he had sought Peace so long and fruitlessly that he was all an itch for action now. He asked questions; and Tope ate his eggs and wagged his head and protested:

"Hold it, Dave, till I'm through. One thing at a time is all I could ever do."

So Howell perforce must wait; till when Tope by and by was done, he told as much as it seemed wise to tell.

"So I'm interested, Dave," he pointed out. "I like Miss Moss, and she's wrapped up in these children, and they're tangled up in this murder thing. So I want to take a hand. But you know Hagan. He doesn't want me around on his heels all the time. And it's Hagan's case, as far as the murder goes."

He hesitated. "But Dave, Peace is in it, somewhere. Peace knew Doctor Canter, and Peace knew Hammond. When Peace wanted to fake that busted foot and the scar on his head, he went to Canter; and when he wanted to disappear, he went to Hammond. So they're all mixed up together."

Howell banged the table. "Sure!"

"Peace is in this," Tope repeated vigorously. "That's my hunch! And if he is, that brings you into it. I want to work with you, Dave. What do you say?"

Howell said grimly: "Whatever you say!"

"We'll work together?"

"Sure!"

Tope nodded briskly, and he stood up and crossed to pay his check. On the sidewalk outside he turned to his companion. "All right, Dave," he said. "Here's the first thing! How much money did Doctor Canter have? How much did he make in the last two years? Where did it come from? Where did it go to? That's what I want to know."

"I can find out," Howell assured him. "But it may take a little while."

"How long?"

"An hour, a week, a month. I can't tell," Dave admitted. "I might get a break."

Tope said seriously: "Dave, hurry!"

"Sure!"

"You can telephone me," the older man directed. "I'm going up to the Jervis Trust to see Miss Moss. You might catch me there!"

And when Howell was gone to do the task assigned, Tope swung away toward Tremont Street; he crossed the street and took the broad walk across the Common. The day was raw and cold as March can be cold in Boston; but the Inspector had no complaints of the weather. He strode along at a surprising speed, his hands swinging at his sides in a fashion almost youthful; and when he came to Tremont Street again, he stopped at a flower shop and bought a blossom for his buttonhole.

He was tempted to take a cluster of flowers to Miss Moss; but his courage would not as yet carry him so far. In fact, as he drew nearer the Jervis Trust offices, he began to be doubtful of this blossom on his lapel; he looked down at it sidewise with an uncertain eye, and his pink cheeks were more pink than usual. Yet he wore it bravely as far as the foot of the stairs that led up to the Trust offices. Then his courage failed, he took it out of his buttonhole, and stood wondering what to do with it, till someone at his elbow said cheerfully:

"Good morning, Inspector!"

It was Miss Moss herself, here beside him. Inspector Tope coughed till he strangled, with sheer embarrassment, and he dropped the small flower, and she picked it up.

"Is it faded?" she asked. "Why no, it's quite fresh. Did you mean to throw it away?"

Inspector Tope's face was crimson, and then he laughed at himself. "Why ma'am," he confessed, "I just bought it. To wear."

"You like flowers?"

"I never thought much about them," the Inspector admitted; but he added, his courage quickening: "Only, this morning, I was on my way to see you!"

She smiled, with a quick dip of her head, as though this were explanation enough, and she said: "Here, wear it, then!" And she replaced it on his lapel. When they went together up the stairs, Tope thought she must hear his heart, it pounded so.

So they came into the Trust offices. Clint was already here. He looked up at their entrance and nodded, and Miss Moss crossed to her desk, the Inspector close beside her. She stripped off her gloves, and she said apologetically:

"I'm late this morning. I stopped in to see Miss Cyr."

"Eh?" Tope asked in surprise. "Oh, yes!"

"She and Mr. Hammond live two floors below us, in our apartment building," Miss Moss reminded him. "You remember, we saw them go in, last night."

"That's right," the Inspector agreed.

"So—I stopped in to see her," Miss Moss repeated. "I was rather touched by her manner last night. She was so terrified —and so brave. With something pitiful in her very courage."

Tope nodded. "How is she?" he asked. "And Hammond? You see him, too?"

"They rise late," Miss Moss confessed. "I suppose all theatrical people do. He was still abed, I think. She was breakfasting, a tray in bed."

Tope's thoughts were always apt to play around the facets of a fact, considering all its implications. "I don't suppose they would have the same bed," he remarked, as though agreeing with something she had said.

"No; separate rooms, evidently," Miss Moss assented. They were sitting at her desk, their tones low. Letters waited her attention here, but she paid no heed to them. The telephone rang, and Clint looked toward her, and she nodded to him so that he came to answer it. And Tope asked:

"Did you find out anything more?"

"I wanted to ask her a question," Miss Moss explained. "It seemed to me important. Of course, I don't know anything about—investigations and such things. But I wanted to ask her whether she knew Doctor Canter was coming, last night."

"Did she?" Tope inquired.

"She expected him to come for her after the performance," Miss Moss told him. "Not before that."

"So she didn't know he'd be there during the second act?"

"No one knew he would be there," Miss Moss agreed. "Until he came. Then of course Mr. Hammond saw him come in, and Clara, and Mr. Hews, and Miss Ransom, and Clint, and others, probably."

Tope looked at his hands where they rested on his knees. He raised his eyes to her and smiled; and he said slowly: "Ma'am, I've told you before, you're miles ahead of me. I can tell, the way you talk, you think this matters; but I don't see why?"

"It must mean two things," she pointed out. "It must mean that the killing wasn't planned in advance, because no one knew Doctor Canter would be there. So the opportunity was an accident. But to seize that opportunity, whoever killed him must have known where the Doctor was, and must have known just when the shooting on the stage would cover the sound of his own shot; and he must have known how to get to Miss Cyr's dressing room without being seen, and how to get away again."

Tope considered, and he nodded slowly. "Yes," he agreed. "Yes, that's so. Someone who meant to kill him, or wanted to kill him, or wished he was dead, saw the chance, and knew how to seize it. That does narrow it down some."

"That narrows it, yes," she said.

"It might have been any one of—several people, at that," he pointed out; and his eyes, following his thought, looked across the room to where Clint had returned to his work, after answering the telephone. Miss Moss saw his glance;

and when he did not speak, she called Clint. The young man came toward them.

"What was the phone call, Clint?" she asked.

The boy reported: "That was Michelsen, up at the apartment. He says they'll need coal by the first of next week. The winter has been cold, so we've used more than usual. The bins are low."

Miss Moss nodded. "Thank you, Clint," she said; and the young man nodded and went back to his files. Miss Moss watched Inspector Tope as his glance followed Clint; and when he turned back to her again she asked with a faint smile:

"You still think he might have done it?"

He chuckled. "What made you think I was—thinking that?"

"He had threatened to kill the Doctor, and he was there, and he knew the routine of the play," she reminded him, and added: "Also, I saw you look at him."

"Ma'am," he protested, "I'll be careful where I look from now on." He shook his head. "No, it wasn't him." And he added: "Nor it wasn't Hammond. Nor Miss Cyr. Nor Hews, nor Miss Jervis."

She said ruefully: "Thank you for that last name. I wish I were sure."

"Aren't you?"

"I was sure last night. Today I'm not."

"You haven't heard from her, or Hews?"

"No," she admitted; and then she smiled. "Nor has Hagan," she added. "There was a policeman outside the apartment this morning; and a man stood across the street watching you and me when we came in here."

"You think she might have?" he insisted. "You think she's capable of it?"

Miss Moss hesitated. "I am thinking about Mat Hews," she confessed. "He loves Clara, and she loves him, I think. In fact, I am sure. But—why did he take her away?"

Tope nodded. "There is that," he admitted.

"Mat tried so hard to take care of her," she reminded him. "You remember at dinner, when Kay started to tell us about Lola's new swain, Mat silenced her. And he told Clara not to come back stage. That was because he was afraid of her meeting Doctor Canter."

The Inspector exclaimed: "That's how you guessed it was Doctor Canter who had been killed!"

She nodded. "It seemed incredible," she admitted. "But I knew it must be he. Instinct, intuition, something."

And she continued: "Then you remember what Miss Cyr said about how Mat hunted all around her dressing room, with his handkerchief in his hand?" Tope assented soundlessly; and she explained: "He saw the gun there, I think, and he knew Clara had had it. So he took his handkerchief and wiped the doorknob, the door jambs, the edge of the dressing table, everything that would take a finger print."

Tope chuckled. "I remember, you told Hagan that," he said.

"Everything he did was done to protect her," Miss Moss urged. "But if she did not do this, it was folly to let her run away."

"That was foolish," Tope confessed. "But the boy might lose his head." He added, smiling faintly: "If I was his age, I'd run away with her myself, if she'd go."

"But don't you see?" Miss Moss insisted miserably. "It means he thinks she did it! It may mean she told him so!"

Tope sat thoughtful for a while, considering this; but in the end he shook his head. "No ma'am" he said at last. "No, you're wrong there. A man don't think the girl he loves did a thing like this." He chuckled. "I'll tell you what they've done!" he declared in a sudden inspiration.

"What?" she asked, a deep concern in her tones.

"They've gone to get married!" Tope predicted. "They'll get married, somewhere, and come back here!"

Miss Moss cried: "This is no time for marrying!"

But the Inspector cheerfully insisted: "The time for marrying is whenever you can talk the right woman into it! Being married is a good thing, ma'am. I've watched people long enough to be sure of that. It's good for a man and for a woman too. It's best if there's some love mixed up in it; but it's good anyway. A man needs a woman, and a woman needs a man. No, any time at all is a good time for marrying."

She said, half to herself: "I have never married. Clara and Clint have been—my children, I suppose."

A moment's silence held them; then he went on: "You see, Mat wouldn't want to have to tell all he knew about Clara, and the gun, and you can't make a husband testify against his wife. Law don't allow it." He chuckled. "Guess the law figures it's better to let a murderer get off than to start a row like that beween a man and his wife. Hews knew the law, I'll bet. Wait and see."

She said doubtfully: "It may be; but it doesn't sound plausible, to me. I don't believe Mat knew anything about such a law. And even if he did, there were others who knew Clara had the gun. Clint and Kay at least. And Kay would certainly tell!"

But Tope urged: "Now ma'am, you're just tormenting yourself. Let's quit worrying and try to figure this out." He spoke more vigorously, anxious to make her forget these fears. "It was someone back stage, someone who belonged back there, who killed Doctor Canter. Hagan will be checking up on them all." His eyes narrowed thoughtfully. "Or it might have been Peace. That notion sticks in my head. You remember anybody in the show that might have been him; anyone the right size?"

She said thoughtfully: "Why, two or three were about his size, I should think. One of the men who worked the machine guns. . . ."

"We'll go again tonight," Tope proposed. "You sit out front. I'll get Dave Howell to take me back. I want to see how the time figures in this; how long it took to shoot the guns; how long after that before Hammond and Miss Cyr would get to her dressing room, and so on. And you watch the people on the stage. If you spot Peace, you can send word back to me."

"I'll try," she agreed.

"Don't think about his looks," Tope warned her. "He could change them, a lot. Just the size, and the voice, and the way he moves his hands and feet." He hesitated, added: "But of course, it's probably someone else. A fellow like this Doctor Canter, he'd make a lot of folks sore at him, living the way he did."

"A woman tried to kill him, out West," she remembered. "I don't know what her name was. . . ."

"We'll find that out," he promised. "I'll telegraph."

The telephone rang again, and Clint looked toward them. But Miss Moss this time lifted the receiver. After a moment she said, in a faint surprise:

"Oh, it's for you."

So Inspector Tope took the phone; and he heard Dave Howell's voice on the wire. He listened, thereafter, for a minute or two; and he said at last:

"Fine, Dave. And Dave, I'll want to see you. Meet me outside here in ten minutes, will you, son."

So he returned the receiver to its hook, and looked at Miss Moss, and wagged his head. She asked:

"What is it?"

"I'm admiring you, ma'am," he told her amiably.

"Why?"

"You mind, you asked me to check up on this Doctor Canter's bank accounts, and all that?"

"Yes."

"Well," said Tope, "Dave Howell has been working on it. He's got something." He hesitated, added then: "Here it is. Two years ago, Peace gave Doctor Canter ten thousand dollars; and a year ago, Peace gave him twenty-two thousand more!"

Miss Moss exclaimed in a quick triumph: "Of course! If Doctor Canter helped Mr. Peace deceive the world about his injuries, he would have to be paid. How did Howell find out?"

Tope explained. "It comes in a funny way," he said. "Dave got it from the Income Tax people. You're not supposed to know that, of course." She nodded with a faint smile.

"What happened," Tope went on. "Doctor Canter didn't return these amounts on his income tax. But Peace did. He put them in as doctor's fees, and professional expenses, because he was on the Trust business at the time he was hurt. The Income Tax people checked up on him because his expense account was so heavy, and he told where the money went. So they got after Canter; and Canter claimed the money was a gift instead of a fee. Afterwards he and Peace got together on their stories; but the mistake they made, they didn't fix it up beforehand. That would have saved all the trouble."

Miss Moss nodded; and Tope added thoughtfully: "The twenty-two thousand was on last year's returns. This year's returns aren't in yet, so we don't know whether Peace paid him any more. But there it is. It proves our guess was right. Peace did fake his bad foot and his busted head, and paid Doctor Canter to back him up. It had to be that way!"

Miss Moss watched him, till suddenly he looked at her.

"And Peace might get tired of paying his bill in instalments like that," he suggested in a low tone.

The woman nodded. She said: "He found a way to get out of the Booth Theatre once without being seen. I wonder if he could use the same way to get in. . . ."

Inspector Tope was late for his rendezvous with Dave Howell outside the Jervis Trust offices; and when he did come down the dingy stairs to meet the other man, he did not tell Dave all that was in his mind. It seemed to him that he and Miss Moss could name the murderer of Doctor Canter; but to do so was useless until Peace was found. So when Tope met Dave Howell, it was not with information but with questions.

"You sure about that stuff on Doctor Canter?" he asked; and when Dave said he was sure, Tope asked, with a sidewise glance at the other man:

"What do you make of it, Dave?"

Howell told him: "Why, Peace must have paid Canter to keep his mouth shut about his foot and his head."

Inspector Tope hesitated; he said at last: "Dave, if we lay hold of the man that killed Canter, we'll be close to the man you're after, too."

"You think it was Peace?"

"I'm guessing so," Tope assented. He added: "But it isn't any easier to find Peace after he's killed a man than it was after he stole that money."

Howell said moodily: "Are you telling me? I've been after him for two months, and him right under my nose!"

Tope retorted soberly: "The chances are he's right under our nose now, Dave. May be an actor in that play; may be a stage hand, anything. It wouldn't surprise me if I'd seen him, talked to him, today.

"And then maybe not. He got out of that theatre without being seen, the night he disappeared. He could get in again just as easy. All we can do is cover every angle. Here's what you do. Go over there this afternoon. See Madison. Check over the list of people in the company. Check over the theatre, the doors and windows back stage and all that. Where could a man hide, for one thing? I saw a lot of big pieces of scenery leaned against the wall; and there's a storeroom on the same floor as the stage; and there must be a basement, and there were galleries up above."

"Sure," Dave assented. "I can do that!"

"And another line," Tope added. "A woman out West tried to shoot this Doctor Canter last fall. Find out who she was, and where she is, and whether she had any relatives that might have taken the job on, and where they are."

"Sure!" Howell agreed. They were passing a drug store; and he said: "Hold up. I'll phone in and have that attended to, right now!"

So Tope waited while the other phoned; and his thoughts were busy ones. He remembered that Miss Moss had talked this morning with Lola Cyr—who was Mrs. Hammond. And so he remembered Hammond; and when Dave came out, the older man said:

"See here, Dave! Let's you and me go talk to Hammond, if he's at home. There was one question that Hagan didn't ask him last night."

And Howell assenting, Tope hailed a taxicab. On the way out to the apartment, the older man explained to Dave what Hammond's part in the affair had been.

"He was on the stage when Canter was shot," Tope pointed out. "So he couldn't have done it. By his own story—I guess it's true—he happened to see Canter's foot sticking out from under the dressing table, and he lost his head and beat it. He saw the gun on the couch; and he saw Canter; but he hid the gun under a pillow, and pushed Canter's foot in out of sight, and took Canter's hat and coat and got out of there. I saw him go; and the time fits."

He added reflectively: "I'm going to the theatre tonight,

Dave, to check up some of those times, while the show is on. But why did Hammond come back? How did he get his nerve back so soon? Most generally, when a man starts running, he keeps on."

"I don't know," Howell confessed.

Tope smiled at the other's tone. "Neither do I," he agreed. "And that's the question Hagan didn't ask him, last night. We'll ask him, if he's home."

And thereafter silence held them till they pulled in to the curb at the apartment. A light snow had begun to fall; and a young man was busy with a broom, clearing the sidewalk in front of the door. A rawboned Scandinavian stood in the vestibule; and Howell said:

"That's Michelsen, the superintendent. I saw him when I came after Peace, the other day." He introduced Michelsen to the Inspector; and Tope asked amiably:

"Got a new janitor, Michelsen, since Burke left you?"

"Yah," said the big man slowly. "I got a man to run the furnaces. His boy helps. That's his boy, sweeping the walk out there."

"Married man, eh?" Tope assented. "You'll find them steadier."

"Sure," Michelsen agreed. "He lives over on Maynard Street."

The two Inspectors passed inside, and Howell turned to look at the names on the panel in the lobby; but before he could ring, Tope said:

"We'll go along up, knock on his door."

The elevator swung them upward, and they found the apartment corresponding to Hammond's card below, and knocked. Annette, the French woman who served Lola as maid, opened to them; and she watched them gravely, and Tope asked whether Hammond were at home. Then the man himself appeared in the passageway behind her, and he recognized Tope and bade them in.

Annette disappeared, and Hammond led the way into the living room of the apartment. Tope, on his heels, saw the slight uncertainty in the man's step; so he was not surprised to discover a bottle, and a glass, and a siphon on the table by the great chair where Hammond must have been sitting.

Hammond was still in his pyjamas and dressing gown; he sat down with a lurch and left them standing; and Tope said:

"You know Inspector Howell, Mr. Hammond. An old friend of mine."

Hammond grinned. "Give your old friend a drink," he suggested. "Take one yourself."

Yet his lips twisted on the words; and his eyes were darting to and fro, and his fingers drummed on the arm of his chair. Inspector Tope thought he was a man beset by fear, strung taut as a wire.

Tope chose a chair and sat down, and Howell balanced his hat upon his knee, and Tope looked blandly about the room, looked back at their host again. He knew a faint pity for Hammond. It was hard to believe that his jangled nerves had no other cause than that one which was known to them all. He said in a sympathetic tone:

"I expect this has been a strain on you."

"Couldn't sleep," Hammond agreed. "Dead for sleep. And a rehearsal this afternoon. Breaking a new juvenile into young Hews' part."

"He's not back?"

"Not him!" Hammond spoke in a deep and furious scorn; yet there was in his tone some hint of secret envy, too.

"Rehearsal this afternoon, eh?" Tope commented. "I might go over with you." Hammond looked at him in surprise and suspicion; and Tope explained: "I meant to go tonight, to time some of the scenes and find out how long it takes for the shooting and so on. But I could go to rehearsal instead."

Hammond shook his head. "It wouldn't do a bit of good," he declared.

"How do you know?" Tope asked sharply; and Hammond started to speak, then changed his mind and was a moment silent before he replied. Sobriety, they saw, began to return to the man, as though his wits were working now.

"I mean, the rehearsal will be stopping and starting, going over and over some scenes and so on," the actor explained. "You can't get the pace from that."

"I see," Tope assented. "And then I expect a new actor will slow things some." Hammond made no comment; and

Tope remarked: "Last night the third act went slower than usual, with Madison in your part."

Hammond said with a faint complacence: "Why yes, I do have to keep the pace up, keep things moving."

"Reminds me," Tope remembered. "I can understand your running away, when you saw Canter dead under the table. But why did you come back, Hammond? Why didn't you keep on running, once you had begun?"

Hammond hesitated. "Didn't see the sense of it," he said then.

"Something stopped you," Tope insisted. "Brought you back. What was it? I'm curious to know."

And Hammond, after a moment, confessed: "Why, Mayhew phoned me." Once he had begun, he explained readily enough. "He's my valet. I skipped out of the theatre and raced home here to grab a bag, to get out of town. He telephoned, told me what had happened, and he said Doctor Canter must have been shot while I was on the stage. So that gave me an alibi, and I decided to go back."

Tope nodded. "Always wished I had a valet!" he reflected, chuckling at his own folly. "This Mayhew must have a good head on him, or he wouldn't have known where to telephone you? Wouldn't have known where you'd be?"

"He thought I was sick, had come home," Hammond explained.

"A man like that would take good care of your clothes," Tope reflected. "Mine surely need it. I bust a button every time I take a deep breath, seems to me. And tying your shoes is hard, when you're old and fat. Yes, sir, if a good fairy was to come along and give me one wish, it'd be a valet I'd wish for." He was smiling at his own words. "Does he press your pants, and tie your ties, and all?" he asked.

Hammond shook his head. "Oh, no," he said impatiently. "I don't use him at home here; just at the theatre. I have to have him for my changes there!"

Tope nodded. "Well," he reflected, "it's a good thing you went back, Hammond. Hagan would have made trouble if you hadn't." He rose. "We'll see you back stage tonight," he said in a friendly tone. "Got to move on now."

Hammond nodded. "Sure," he assented. "I'll be there."

He did not rise to see them go. When Tope looked back from the door the man was still sprawling in his big chair. Dave and Tope went out and closed the door behind them; they walked in silence to the elevator; they came to the street and moved aimlessly away.

They had walked a block or so before Tope turned to the other man.

"Well, Dave," he asked, "what do you think of Hammond?"

"A drunken bum," said Howell.

"More than that, son," Tope said soberly. "He's scared! Scared to death!" He gripped Dave's arm in an emphatic gesture. "Dave," he asked, "why should Hammond be scared?"

"Think he did this?" Dave countered.

But Tope shook his head. "Not sure what I do think, son," he confessed. He stopped still, spoke soberly. "You go along, Dave," he said. "I'm going to walk up and down and let my head settle." He considered. "You get the stuff I told you about. The woman out West, Madison at the theatre, whatever you can about Canter. I'll meet you in the Booth lobby at eight. Right?"

"Sure," Howell agreed.

"And if you see Hagan, don't tell him anything," Tope suggested. But Dave exploded:

"I don't know anything! I'm walking in a fog!"

The old man nodded his amused approval. "Well, that's fine, Dave," he declared. "That's fine!"

Howell grinned ruefully and turned away. When he was gone, Tope drifted for a while. The light snow still persisted; the small flakes brushed his cheeks. The air was still so that the snow fell straight down, and it was not uncomfortably cold. So Tope instead of taking cab or subway, walked down town till he came home again to his room on Boylston Street. He kindled a fire in the grate, and when it was burning freely he telephoned the Jervis Trust. Miss Moss spoke with him. There was no news of Clara, she said.

"I was thinking," Tope suggested, "we might have dinner together, before the theatre. Clint too, if he wants to come."

He hesitated. "Unless he'd better stay home and wait for some word from his sister."

He thought there was faint mirth in her tones. "Why, yes," she assented. "I will be glad to dine with you. But Clint will probably stay at home."

So he made arrangements for their meeting; and thereafter Tope stayed alone in his room, considering and assorting the disordered facts he had accumulated during the hours since Doctor Canter was found under Lola's dressing table the night before. He sat in his great chair before the fire, and he was warm and comfortable; so he slept at last and he roused at dusk, and waked to dress hurriedly and go to meet Miss Moss.

This time, he ventured to buy a corsage for her at the flower shop in the hotel lobby; and when she came in, he presented it with a chuckle.

"I'm laughing at myself, ma'am," he confessed. "But I've found out one thing, in my time. If you want to do a thing, and can do it, you'd better. Then you'll have it to remember, and no one can take it away from you. And I kind of wanted to give you these."

She was pinning the small cluster of violets at her waist; her cheeks were bright. "I'm glad you wanted to," she said frankly.

"Don't know as I ever did give a lady flowers before," he admitted; and she smiled at him with amused and mischievous eyes.

"Don't know as I ever had flowers from a gentleman before," she confessed in mimicry of his own tones; and he offered her his arm with an ease which surprised himself.

"Then it's time we both began," he declared.

They chose to patronize the main dining-room. "Dinner and flowers and the theatre," he remarked, as they went in. "I'll have to get us a box of candy by and by. This is a real party, for me, ma'am."

But Miss Moss said, almost regretfully: "I'm going to disappoint you about the theatre, Inspector. Clara telephoned. She's coming home."

He forgot all else instantly in this intelligence. "When?" he asked.

"I had the message when I went home to dress," she explained. "I do my own work when I'm alone there; and Clara likes fussing around the kitchen, so we have no maid. This was just a message from the switchboard operator downstairs. Clara had phoned that she would be home tonight. That's all we know."

Tope nodded. "I'd like to be with you when she comes," he suggested at last. "See what she says. . . . If you wouldn't mind. And we'll let the theatre go!"

"I was hoping you'd suggest that," she agreed.

They ordered dinner; and they spoke of each other for a while and forgot these sober matters altogether. When they had dined, Tope remembered that he was to meet Howell at the theatre; so they stopped there while he told Dave what to do in his absence. Then Tope and Miss Moss drove out to the apartment building on the Avenue.

They found Clint there; but he had no new word from Clara, so they settled themselves to wait in a momentary expectation of the girl's appearance. But for a long while she did not come, and the hours dragged. Clint suggested three-handed bridge, but Inspector Tope knew nothing of the game. So Miss Moss and Clint began to teach him backgammon, and the old man showed a shrewd appreciation of the strategy and tactics of this pastime, combining discreet retreat with bold audacity so well that he began to win an occasional game from them by and by.

The evening slipped away, and eleven struck, and twelve. Clint became increasingly restless; and even Miss Moss began to be in some degree uneasy. Tope was outwardly serene; yet his composure was only superficial. He thought Clara might have met some mischance; he wondered whether Mat Hews were with her; and he was conscious that the hour was late, and that Miss Moss might be wishing he would go home. Yet he waited stubbornly; and when at about a quarter of one they heard a faint tap at the door, he knew a vast relief. He and Miss Moss were on their feet upon the instant; but Clint was at the door before them, swung it wide.

Clara, and young Hews, came darting in; they were laughing softly together; they looked back over their shoulders; they spoke in gay whispers, hands entwined.

"H-sh!" Clara bade them. "We sneaked in! There was a great big policeman watching outside to nab me!"

Tope looked at Miss Moss, and he saw tears in her eyes. Then Clara saw these tears too, and she was suddenly contrite, and she fled to the older woman, caught her close.

"Darling!" she cried. "Did you worry terribly? I'm sorry. I really am."

Miss Moss smiled mistily. "Sorry nonsense!" she retorted. "You're the least sorry-looking young people I ever saw in my life! Both of you, happy as clams!"

"Clams?" Clara protested, shuddering with mirth. "I'm not a clam. Nor Mat!" She reached behind her, hooked her hand through Mat's arm, drew him forward. "Look at him, darling," she commanded. "Clint, you too." She even included Inspector Tope. "And you! You're a nice old thing. Don't you think he's nice, too?"

Mat grinned in a vast discomfort; and Miss Moss turned to him.

"My dear," she said understandingly, "I always liked you. Here!" She rose on tiptoe to kiss him.

And Clint stared at one of them and the other. "Say, what's it all about?" he protested; and then he laughed aloud and clapped Mat Hews on the shoulder.

"Done it?" he cried.

"Done it," Clara told them jubilantly. "This morning, early. In the most darling little town. An old minister with lovely whiskers, and a hired man and the minister's wife. She gave us griddle cakes for breakfast. And we drove home slowly, through the snow."

Mat said soberly: "I wanted you there, Miss Moss. And Clint too! But—it seemed like the thing to do; the thing for us to do."

Clara cried: "It was all perfectly thrilling from the start!" And Miss Moss said smilingly:

"We don't know anything at all, remember. Start at the beginning, dear!"

Clara looked at Mat with dancing eyes. "Well, the beginning was a fearful row!" she confessed, laughing at the memory. "You see, Mat had found his pistol in Lola's dressing room; and he knew I'd taken it, and he thought of course I killed Doctor Canter . . ."

Mat protested gravely: "I thought you were a darned little fool for taking the gun, and lying to Hagan, and going to Lola's dressing room to quarrel some more with Canter!"

"Well anyway," Clara insisted, "he took me into his dressing room to scold me, and I was furious with him; and then he started to climb out of the window. . . ."

"I wanted to get rid of that gun." Mat explained. "Before they found it and hooked it up with Clara."

"But we weren't nearly through with our fight." Clara took up the tale. "So when he jumped out of the window I jumped after him; and when he climbed into his car, so did I. And he tried to put me out, and I raged at him, and we had a frightful row, and he was driving like mad all the time. And then all of a sudden we made up. . . ." Her eyes turned to Mat. "And after that," she said softly, "everything was beautiful! And coming home was so darned exciting; with policemen everywhere. There was one out front here! We had to sneak in through the alley and the cellar to get here at all. Came up in the freight elevator!"

"Why not the regular elevator, or the stairs?" Miss Moss asked, for the sake of watching the girl's happy countenance.

"Well, the freight elevator was already down there, with a light on, and the door open," Clara told them. She laughed at the recollection. "We had a time with it. Mat couldn't start it; and then he couldn't stop it. If this hadn't been the very top floor, we couldn't have stopped; but it wouldn't go any higher!"

Miss Moss said then, smilingly: "Clara, I don't blame you for running away with this young man—so long as you're back again. But dear, we want to find out some things from you."

Clara's eyes clouded. "I suppose so," she agreed. "Even Mat cross-examined me!" She looked at him in a gay reproach.

"I sure was dumb," said the young man regretfully.

Inspector Tope spoke for the first time. "You can't be blamed much, Hews," he said. "You knew enough to make anyone—think just what you thought. Only I wouldn't have had the nerve to wipe out her finger prints, in the dressing room!"

Mat stared at him; but Clara whispered: "Did you, Mat? Did you do that? You didn't tell me! Darling!" She was a moment silent; and her eyes communed with his. She said then to them all:

"But I didn't have the gun! I had laid it down on the props table in the wings. I meant to give it back to Mat when he came off; but I forgot to look for it again!"

"You did go to speak to Doctor Canter?" Miss Moss asked.

"Yes," she assented reluctantly. "Yes, I . . ."

But they were interrupted by a sharp, broken knock on the door; a knock that was somehow eloquent of frantic haste. It was Inspector Tope this time who opened, while the others stood paralyzed.

He opened the door and a woman came stumbling in; a woman in her nightdress, with staring, tear-dimmed eyes, and cheeks streaked with tears, and scant brown hair of a dingy, lifeless hue. A woman shuddering with racking fears. She stumbled past Inspector Tope, into this room. . . .

And it was only when her back was turned that he realized she wore over her nightgown a negligee of metal cloth, bright as silver. This was Lola Cyr!

She was no beauty now; a distracted woman, nothing more. Her dull brown hair hung in a thin braid a few inches down her back. She looked to right and left; and she asked sharply:

"Is Walter here?"

Hammond was not here; so much was palpable. Their silence answered her.

She cried: "I don't know where he is! I'm afraid!"

Miss Moss drew near her, touched her arm reassuringly. "What is it?" she asked. "Tell us, please."

"I thought he'd gone to bed long ago," the woman whispered. "Annette was rubbing me. I went into his room, and he was gone; and the elevator man says he didn't go down. I thought he might be here!"

And she added hopelessly: "He was undressed! His clothes are there! Where has he gone?"

Clint protested: "He couldn't get out, any other way except the elevator!"

But Inspector Tope moved nearer. "You stay here," he told the trembling woman gently. He spoke to Miss Moss and Clara: "You folks take care of her. We'll find him!"

And he summoned Clint and young Mat Hews with his eyes. They stepped out into the hall. He spoke to Mat.

"You said the freight elevator was down in the cellar," he reminded that young man. "Where is it now? He might have gone that way!"

"I'll show you," Mat answered. "But—what was Hammond doing with her? That's Lola Cyr! Say, she's not bald at all, is she? Not even beautiful!"

"They're married! She loves him!" Tope spoke sharply. "And—the man was afraid of death today! Hurry, son."

So Mat was silenced, and these three moved swiftly down the hall. They stepped into the freight elevator and descended; they emerged into the dark cavern of the cellar.

Here were long shadowed corridors flanked by boarded cubbies in which lodgers might store their trunks or extra furniture. At the end of the passage on the right, a single light glowed dimly. Tope hesitated.

"Was the outside door unlocked?" he asked Mat. "How did you get in?"

"Unlocked, yes," said young Hews. "But shut!"

"Hammond wouldn't go out in his pyjamas," Tope considered. "Let's look around, see if he's here!"

So they began a methodic search of the cellar. They found the switchboard and turned on every light. Inspector Tope walked ahead; the two younger men moved furtively upon his heels, their nerves drawn tight.

They found Walter Hammond in one of the coal bins. This was a huge concrete vault, the floor sloping downward toward the door at which they entered. A naked bulb hung from the ceiling to illumine the place. In its further end, a heap of fine coal, half a dozen tons or so, reflected the light in faint gleaming points. Halfway from the door to this mound of coal, Hammond lay.

Tope bade the others wait in the door; he approached the man, knelt beside him, struck a match.

Hammond was in his pyjamas and dressing gown, the garments he had worn that morning when Tope and Howell called upon him. His hands were black with coal dust. He was all begrimed with it. He sprawled on his back and he was dead. A wadded blanket lay beside him on the black floor.

Tope saw that one of the bullets had passed through the man's wrist, as though Hammond had flung out his hand to ward off the death he saw imminent. The bullet had smashed his watch; the hands had stopped at twenty-two minutes of one.

The Inspector, kneeling there, looked at his own watch. It was now just past one o'clock. He remembered that at about twenty-two minutes of one, Clara and Mat Hews must have been in this cellar on their way upstairs; and for a moment as he crouched above the murdered man, Tope felt himself unutterably weary and old.

9

INSPECTOR TOPE could act quickly when there was need of quick action; but also he could wait to set his thoughts in order. He did so now. By the watch on Hammond's wrist, the man had been shot at twenty-two minutes of one. Mat and Clara, on their own statement, had been here in the cellar at about that time. Tope estimated that they had been upstairs perhaps fifteen minutes before Lola knocked on the door; it might have required another five minutes for the Inspector and Mat and Clint to come down and search, and find Hammond here. . . . And it was now five minutes past one. Then twenty-five minutes ago, Mat and Clara must have been about entering the cellar.

But Tope returned to sanity again, even while he stayed kneeling beside the dead man, his back turned toward the doorway where Clint and Mat stood watching. Murder was not in these youngsters. He remembered how their eyes shone when they came into the room upstairs; he remembered their bright cheeks, and quick laughter, and gay mirthful tones. Not they.

Then Clint asked, behind him, in a husky voice: "Is he dead?"

Tope nodded. "Wait," he muttered. He was thinking, still. Perhaps they had come through the cellar while the slayer still lurked in some shadow here. They might even have heard the shot. He asked:

"Mat? You hear anything when you were down here? See anyone? How long were you here?"

Mat said quickly: "No. Not a soul. Not even in the alley. We went from the outer door straight through to the elevator; saw the door open, and the light on, and went straight through. No, we didn't hear a thing!"

"Hear anything while you were still outside, before you came in?" Tope insisted.

"No."

Yet the night was still, the air unstirring. On such a night sounds carry far. Strange that they had not heard the shot, even in the alley; strange that no one on the first floor had heard. The Inspector's glance cast to and fro; and he saw the crumpled blanket tossed beside the body on the concrete floor.

He touched the blanket gingerly with his forefinger, opening the folds, careful not to disturb it too much; and so he found at last that which he had counted on discovering. A small, charred hole; a smut of burned powder. The murderer had muffled his gun in this blanket before he fired, to deaden the sound.

Tope looked at the dead man intently. One bullet had struck his wrist, on the inner side, and smashed through between the bones and battered the wrist watch into shapelessness. That was the ball, Tope judged, which had hit Hammond in the face. The wound was there. But another had pierced his chest; and there were faint powder marks upon his bright pyjamas. And the Inspector tilted back on his heels to consider these matters. The first shot had been fired then from a little distance, through Hammond's upflung wrist, into his face. That would have stunned him, perhaps killed him, at least knocked him down. The second shot was at close range; a mercy stroke to the wounded man.

Yet there was something here that offended the Inspector's instinct for the fitness and symmetry of things. He could not set his finger on the point which puzzled him; neverthless it remained lurking in his mind.

But in the meantime, there was a punctilio to be observed. Tope rose and backed carefully out of the vaulted concrete chamber in which Hammond lay. There might be other footprints in the coal dust here, of some significance. He backed to the door, and the younger men drew aside to let him through, and he saw their white faces, saw their eyeballs gleam in the naked light.

Clint whispered: "What do you make of it, Inspector?"

But Tope wagged his head. "Not time to think about that, yet," he returned. He spoke to these youngsters with authority. "Clint, you go out and find a policeman. Bring him here. Tell him I'm here and I'm notifying Headquarters, so he needn't stop to phone."

"Right," Clint assented briskly; he turned away.

And Tope said to young Hews: "Son, you stay here, by the door."

"All right, sir," Hews agreed. "But—shouldn't someone take word upstairs?"

"I'll go up with you presently," Tope told him. "You wait now."

So Hews waited; and the Inspector went searching for a phone. He set about this like a man who knew his ground; and he smiled grimly, remembering how he knew where now to look for what he sought. Peace in his character of Burke had lived in this basement, in a room off the furnace room; and Tope guessed that there must be in this room a telephone. Else how could Miss Moss have warned Peace that the time had come for him to flee?

He found the room, he found the telephone, he called Headquarters to report what had happened here. And: "Tell Hagan," he directed, "that this hooks up with the Canter case. He'll want to come."

Having done this, he turned his attention to the room in which he stood. It was disused now, he remembered. Michelsen had told them the day before that the janitor who took Burke's job slept at home. Tope saw a bed, a table, some books and magazines, a chair or two. The bed was disordered where a blanket had been torn away. That would be the blanket which lay now on the floor beside the dead man.

There was a window which opened into a sunken area off the alley, and Tope found this window unlatched, and he opened it to look out. But there were no traces in the smooth snow. The murderer, Tope reflected, had had no need to use this method of entrance, since the alley door was, according to Mat, unlocked.

And he wondered suddenly whether the killer were gone; and he stood still a moment at the thought. He was not a fearful man, yet there were fears in him now. This individual with whom they had to deal, Peace or some other, possessed a cool ferocity not easily to be turned aside. To have killed once is to acquire a sort of immunity; when your own life is already forfeit, to kill and kill again does not increase the penalty of capture. Doctor Canter was dead, and Hammond was dead; and unless the killer were laid promptly by the heels, others well might die. If the man had even minor reasons for another killing, he need not now hesitate through any fear of punishment. Only the risk of detection could deter him.

But this same fear of capture might prompt him to kill again, in a sort of self-defense. Suppose he were somewhere here; hidden, watching, waiting to escape. . . . Tope moved briskly out into the furnace room again; he crossed to where young Hews stood by the entrance to that coal bin where the body lay, and he felt something like relief to find the youngster safe and sound.

"All right?" he asked. "See anyone? Hear anyone?"

Hews shook his head. "I'd like to go upstairs, sir," he urged. "They'll be frantic."

"In a minute," Tope promised. "Wait till Clint comes."

Mat fretted at the delay; but they had not long to wait before Clint returned with an officer. He was unknown to Tope, but he had heard the Inspector's name. Tope told him briefly:

"The body's in there! Walter Hammond, the actor. He's

been playing in that gangster thing at the Booth. I've telephoned Headquarters. Hagan must be on the way."

"Right, Inspector," the policeman agreed.

Tope explained: "Everything's just the way it was." He pointed to the floor. "Tell Hagan those are my tracks, in the coal dust. I walked in to look at him, and backed out. He may find other tracks besides mine."

"You find anything?"

Tope hesitated. "I looked around," he confessed. "Hagan may want to talk to me. Tell him I'm upstairs, Apartment 14-A." And he added: "I'll see to it there's someone to let him in when he comes."

The younger man saluted; and Tope, with Clint and young Hews at his heels, found the stairs that led up to the first floor. They discovered the elevator man asleep in a chair at the telephone switchboard, since this was during the small hours of the night also in his charge. They roused him and bade him watch for Hagan's coming, and then Tope and the others stepped into the elevator and the man ran them to the fourteenth floor. In the corridor outside the door of the apartment, Tope warned the younger men to let him do the talking. Then he knocked, and Miss Moss opened the door.

Lola Cyr sat yonder on the couch, leaning forward, pale and intent upon his first word; and Tope found it hard to believe that this rather plain woman with dull, scant hair could when she chose present such beauty to the world. He stood uncertainly, and Clara came swiftly to Mat's side, caught him in her arms; and Miss Moss looked her question.

Inspector Tope spoke to the actress. "I'm sorry, ma'am. He's dead," he said simply.

He saw the blood drain out of her lips. Her lips parted, and closed, and parted again. Then a keen, small sound like a wail issued from them; a hopeless cry like that of a feeble infant. She toppled slowly forward, and before they could come to her she had collapsed, her head striking with a thump upon the hardwood floor between the rugs.

Clint and the Inspector lifted her back upon the couch again, and Miss Moss directed: "Let her head hang down, over the edge of the couch. That will revive her."

Tope shifted the woman's inert body, obediently; and he

stepped back to yield his place to Miss Moss. She sent Clara for water, and a moment later, while she was moistening Lola's brow, she said over her shoulder to the Inspector:

"She and Mr. Hammond were late leaving the theatre. He had an argument with his valet, discharged the man. That delayed them; but they got home about eleven-thirty or a little later. Annette came with them."

Tope nodded intently; and she continued:

"Annette gives Mrs. Hammond a rub, a massage every night for an hour. Mr. Hammond went to his own room, just after they came home, and she didn't see him again."

"When was it she missed him?"

"After Annette finished with her. That would make it about half-past twelve or later. She went in to say good night to him."

Lola's eyes opened; she moaned: "He was gone!"

"I was telling the Inspector," Miss Moss explained.

"I couldn't find him," the woman whispered. "I telephoned downstairs and no one had seen him. So I came up to you."

"Up in the elevator?" Tope asked.

Miss Moss said: "She ran up the fire stairs!"

He nodded: "Where's Annette?"

"She goes home at night," Miss Moss explained.

"Hagan will want her," Tope suggested. "Where does she live? And he'll want to talk to the valet, too. About that argument." He asked the weeping woman: "You know where they live?"

"Annette's at a hotel," Lola told him, and named the hostelry. "I think Mayhew boards, somewhere in the South End. I don't know where. I've heard Walter telephone him."

"Remember the number?" Tope asked.

She did, and repeated it; and he made a note of it. "I'll go check up with the operator," he decided. "Find out the address, in case Inspector Hagan wants it. You all can take care of her?"

"Of course," Miss Moss assured him.

Inspector Tope might have used the telephone in the room; but on second thought he went out and rang for the elevator. Inspector Hagan, he found, had not yet arrived. Belowstairs, Tope sat down at the switchboard, and a minute's conversation brought him the information he desired. Then it occurred to him that he need not wait for Hagan. There was an angry impatience in him now. Mayhew's boarding house was not a mile away; and Tope was suddenly alert to see this man.

A taxi, the driver sleeping, stood at the curb. Inspector Tope woke him, and a few minutes later the cab pulled up before a house, one of a block of houses each exactly alike; and the Inspector got out. He ascended the steps and rang the bell.

He had to wait some time before an answer came. Then a woman in a dingy bathrobe opened the door to him, grumbling and sleepy-eyed. She muttered something; and he said briskly:

"Sorry to wake you up, ma'am. A gentleman named Mayhew boards here?"

"Yes," she told him.

"Home, is he?"

"Came in a little while ago," she admitted. "Lost his latchkey; and he waked me up to let him in. I like my sleep of nights. If he's going to have visitors this time of night, he can move out of my house!"

Tope hesitated: "Late getting home, was he?"

"Quarter past twelve," she said irascibly. "His watch had stopped, and he set it by mine. I told him if he lost his key again, he'd get in earlier hereafter, or stay out all night."

Tope nodded in a slow disappointment. "I guess I won't wake him up, then, ma'am," he decided. "I'll see him tomorrow, instead." He heard her angry comment on the idiocy of rousing a respectable woman at this time of night and then changing your mind about a thing; but he made no retort. He was curiously depressed by this intelligence that Mayhew had been safe at home a full twenty minutes before Hammond was killed. That instinct of his upon which he had learned more and more to rely had quickened into life when he heard that Mayhew and Hammond tonight had argued on some matter unknown.

His cab was waiting; he came back again to the apartment. Hagan must have arrived; for there was a police car before the door, and Doctor Gero's automobile just behind it. Tope hesitated, half minded to go down cellar and join them. But Inspector Hagan would resent his presence there. And—Tope wished to see Miss Moss again.

So he took the elevator to their floor. He found that they had put Lola Cyr to bed.

"I gave her a bromide," Miss Moss confessed. "Poor thing; she is so stricken. She is sleeping now."

Clara and Mat Hews were together on the couch, their arms entwined. It was Clint who asked the Inspector: "Where have you been?"

"Checking up," the old man said, a little wearily. He looked at Miss Moss and explained: "I went to see where Mayhew lives. I had a sort of feeling about him, a hunch." He grinned, wagged his head. "Used to trust my hunches, but I'm getting old."

"Why?" she asked.

And he told her: "Hammond was killed about twelve-thirty-five. But Mayhew was home at a quarter past twelve."

"How do you know?" she wondered.

"His landlady had to let him in. She was mad about it. He'd lost his latchkey."

"I mean, about Mr. Hammond?" she corrected; and he said:

"Oh, a bullet hit his watch and stopped it."

She considered this. "I see." And after a moment: "But Inspector. . . ."

But before she could finish what she had begun to say, there came heavy footfalls outside the door, and a harsh knock there. Clint opened, and Inspector Hagan, with a uniformed policeman behind him, strode into the room.

He said harshly: "Hullo, Tope. They told me that you. . . ." Then he saw Clara, and young Hews here, and his face crimsoned. "Ha!" he exclaimed. "This where you've been hiding, is it?" He whirled on Tope. "You knew it! Knew I wanted them."

But young Hews cried: "He didn't! We haven't been here!"

And Clara, on her feet, that quick temper of hers flaming in her eyes, exclaimed: "No one knew anything, except us! We just came."

"Just came?" Hagan echoed.

"Tonight."

"How did you get in? My men didn't see you."

"Through the cellar!"

Hagan's eyes narrowed. "What time was that?" he asked, more quietly; and Tope made a quick forward movement. But Hagan swung toward him warningly, and Tope held his tongue, and Clara said frankly:

"About half-past twelve or quarter of one. Just a little while ago."

Inspector Hagan nodded, and his eyes were shining. "Why, that's fine," he declared. "That fits right in. I'm glad to know that, young lady."

Clara recoiled, puzzled and uneasy; he took a step toward her. But Miss Moss came between.

"What of it, Inspector?" she asked crisply.

"Hammond was killed at twelve-thirty-eight," he told her. "In the cellar. And they were there! That's what of it. That's good enough for me."

"Nonsense," Miss Moss protested; and Hagan said furiously:

"Is that so? All right, here's some more nonsense! She hated Canter, and she had a gun, and she went in to the dressing room where he was. Stage hand saw her go in. Saw her come out, too, and hide behind some scenery. He came and told me about it after you left, that night."

"I was crying!" Clara told him unhappily. "I didn't want anyone to see me cry, so I hid."

"But you left the gun behind," he said, his voice rising. "You went back and got it, afterward."

Mat Hews stood by her side. "No, I took the gun, Inspector," he corrected.

"Where is it?"

The boy grinned: "In the river! I threw it over the rail when we drove across the bridge!"

"You're the one she ran away with?"

"Yes."

"Where'd you go?"

"To get married," said Mat steadily; and his arm encircled her.

"Ho!" Hagan's mirth was not appealing. "Married, eh? Well, you'll honeymoon in jail! Maybe I can give you a double cell. I'll see." He turned to the officer beside him. "O'Malley, we'll take them along!"

But Miss Moss stepped in front of O'Malley as he moved forward; she spoke to Hagan. "You're absurd, Inspector," she said sharply. "You'll do nothing of the kind!"

"That so?" he echoed in a sardonic tone; yet he seemed somehow abashed. He hesitated, and when he spoke again it was almost persuasively.

"Why, here it is," he urged. "You folks can see it's reasonable, too. Maybe I'm wrong, but everything I know points to her, and to young Hews here. It's my job not to take chances. I've got to hold the both of them."

Miss Moss retorted: "You won't hold them twelve hours. I'll have a *habeas corpus* on your back before you get to Headquarters. Inspector, you're a fool! Any man's a fool where women are concerned, but you're worse than most! Any woman can see with half an eye that Clara had nothing to do with this, nor Mat. They haven't a thought but each other."

"You can see more than I can!" he protested.

"Of course I can!" she agreed. "You're blind as a bull bat, my friend." Her eyes were bright, her tones were curt; and Inspector Tope watched her with a deep approval.

"I suppose you know who did this?" Hagan challenged.

She shook her head. "I know no more than you, so far as facts are concerned. I say no word but this. If you molest Clara here, or this boy, I'll make you the laughingstock of the city. I'll laugh you out of the Force."

He hesitated; and she said summarily: "You're a boor, and a clown and a dunce! I don't know how you ever got where you are. Your intelligence is nil, and your manners are unbearable. Now get out of my apartment; and when you come again, bring a warrant to enter, and carry your hat in your hand."

Inspector Hagan, with a ludicrous haste, snatched off his hat. He said apologetically: "Why, ma'am, I'm doing the best I know."

"You know enough to take your hat off."

"I'm sorry about that. I wasn't thinking about hats."

"It's time you did," she said. "Now walk yourself out of here."

He hesitated, and he looked appealingly at Tope. But Inspector Tope with a great indifference let his glance wander around the room, and Hagan, denied even this much support, moved reluctantly toward the door. But on the threshold there he paused.

"Just the same, ma'am," he said harshly, "you all stay here! I'll be keeping an eye on you."

"Of course we'll stay, you idiot!" she told him. "This is where we live."

And she moved toward him so vigorously that Hagan in something like a panic abruptly backed out of the room and shut the door.

Miss Moss saw him go; and she whirled and set her shoulders against the door and leaned there, suddenly weak and shaken. Clara ran toward her in a swift delight; the girl cried: "You old darling, you're a marvel!"

Miss Moss smiled weakly. "I've taken care of you and Clint so long, child. I'm like a hen fighting for her chicks!"

"I'm sorry," Clara whispered. "I got us all in this mess! I'm a little fool. . . ."

But Inspector Tope said cheerfully: "Now Mrs. Hews, you go over there with your new husband. I've a notion Miss Moss has a word to say to me."

And Clara looked at them, and suddenly she smiled. "You two!" she laughed. "Always whispering like conspirators!" She drew away.

Tope saw that Miss Moss was blushing at Clara's amusement; and his own ears burned. But Miss Moss asked, to hide her own confusion:

"Why did you think I've something. . . ."

"You started to say it just before Hagan came," he reminded her.

"Oh?" She was silent, seeking to remember. "Oh, yes," she said then. "About the time Mr. Hammond was killed, and the watch. I was thinking, sometimes watches might be wrong!"

Tope nodded briefly: "That's so. But, ma'am, I'm thinking about something else now." He hesitated, brought the matter out into the light: "Day before yesterday, the day Howell came up here to get Peace, and Peace was gone. You . . ."

"I telephoned him, yes," she assented.

"Call him by name?"

"No, no. I told him Inspector Howell was coming up to find out whether he knew anything about Peace. No, I called him Burke. But of course he would understand."

"How did you know Howell would be coming up here?"

"I guessed from your questions," she confessed. "It was clear that you—suspected something; and you would tell Howell."

He nodded, frowning at his own thoughts; the expression of concern was strange to see on his calm countenance. "But here it is," he said. "Even if you didn't call him by name, he'd know that you knew him, knew he was Peace."

"Why?" she asked. "I suppose he would, but I don't see . . ."

"Ma'am," he insisted soberly. "You're a grown woman, you can listen. If Peace killed the doctor and Hammond, he won't mind another killing. And if he killed them, it was because they knew him, could give him away. Well, you knew him, too!"

She understood. "But I'm not afraid!" she said. "And he might even be grateful for my warning."

Inspector Tope urged: "It's more likely he figures you were the one gave him away."

"If I hadn't warned him," Miss Moss reflected wearily, "Inspector Howell would have caught him that day. And—Doctor Canter, and Mr. Hammond would still be alive. I blame myself. But I was thinking of the children!"

He shook his head. "Ma'am, you're not to worry about that," he advised her. "Maybe they had it coming. And anyway, no one can do better than his best. You did the thing that seemed best to you then. Don't go regretting it now."

She said gently: "You find, always, some reassuring word. Thank you!"

And Inspector Tope colored with pleasure; but he insisted:

"The thing is—I'm afraid for you. I'm asking you to let me stay the night right here."

Miss Moss considered; and she smiled. "We're already crowded!" she reminded him. "With a new bride and groom to be made comfortable; and Miss Cyr in the guest room. I can only give you a blanket on the couch, Inspector?"

"I don't aim to sleep," he assured her.

"Why then, I might sit and keep you company," she offered.

He said huskily: "I'd admire that, ma'am. I'd like that, if you would. . . ."

Lola Cyr was long since asleep, but these others were in no haste to be abed. Clara and Mat had so much to tell, so much to ask. They sat side by side on the broad couch, very close together; and Clint laughed at their eager ardor now and then, and he protested once to Clara:

"Leave him alone for a minute, can't you sis! Keep your hands off him. You act like a kid with a new doll. His tie's all right, and so's his hair!"

"Well, I don't care," Clara declared in a laughing pride. "I have to take care of him! He's always so rumpled!"

Mat chuckled happily. "She mended a hole in my socks this morning," he told them. "And she'd have sewed a button on, if there'd been one that needed it."

They chattered cheerfully together, in the quick forgetfulness of youth already neglecting that tragedy which had stalked so near them, touched them with its shadow passing by. But they came back to it at last; this death of Hammond; that of Doctor Canter. And Miss Moss asked Clara a question, and Clint and Mat supplemented her reply, so that between them they gave some orderly account of what had happened back stage on the night of Doctor Canter's death. Tope, listening, sought to assort the matter in his mind.

It assumed a smooth chronology. First the four young folk were in the dressing room; Clara with Kay, Clint with Mat. Then Clara and Kay crossed to join the two young men; and Clara saw the pistol in Mat's dressing table drawer, and picked it up and would not give it back to him.

"Why not?" Miss Moss asked; and Clara's cheeks were bright.

"Clint was so superior about it," she confessed. "And—I wanted Mat to—to sort of chase me." She was laughing at her own folly. "I wanted him to take it away from me." She looked at Mat, and added mischievously. "I'd been trying to drive him to violence, or something, for weeks. He's the slowest man!"

And they laughed at her and with her; then drew soberly back once more to the matter here in hand.

She and Mat were tussling in the corridor outside the dressing room, the others cheering them on, when Doctor Canter came up the steps from the stage door. When he was about to pass them, Clara recognized him, cried his name; and Clint swung furiously toward the man. So they had some swift, hot words, Clint angry, Doctor Canter mocking him, Clara blind with rage!

"I wanted to just—slap him," Clara declared. "Only I was so mad I couldn't move!"

Then suddenly there was the curtain, and Mat and Kay must go on. Clint and Clara followed them as far as the entrance; but Clara watched Doctor Canter. She saw him pause outside Walter Hammond's door.

"Mr. Hammond's man spoke to him," she said. "And then Mr. Hammond came out, and he and Doctor Canter talked a minute, and then Doctor Canter laughed in that nasty way he had, and went on."

She said she had no thought at the time of following him; but later, Lola came to join Hammond for their entrance; and at the same time Annette went out to the stairs to go down cellar. The angular maid's dislike of firearms was a standing joke in the company. Seeing her go, Clara realized that Doctor Canter must be alone; and she turned irresistibly that way, driven by the fury his mocking mirth had a while ago aroused.

Miss Moss interrupted her at this point to ask: "Where was the pistol, Clara?"

"Oh, I had already put it down. There's a props table back of the drop, right by Mr. Hammond's door," she explained. "I laid it down there, while Clint was talking to Doctor Canter, when he first came in."

"Was that wise? Someone might have picked it up, fired it accidentally."

"I wasn't thinking," Clara explained. "I was so mad I couldn't. Then when I remembered and looked for it, it was gone. I supposed the props man had found it. He'd spot it in a minute if it didn't belong on the table, you know!"

Miss Moss inquired: "When was it you looked for it, found it gone?"

"Just after the curtain."

"Where was Doctor Canter then?"

"By Mr. Hammond's dressing room. Just outside the door."

Tope asked quickly: "Then someone had picked it up after you laid it down and before Doctor Canter left Hammond and went on to Miss Cyr's dressing room!"

"Yes," Clara answered. "Yes, I'm sure! It was gone!"

Tope nodded, and she went on to tell how she confronted Canter in Lola's dressing room, striking out at him blindly with lashing tongue.

"He was so hateful!" she cried. "So contemptible! I don't know what I said; but he laughed at me, and I got so mad I began to cry. So I ran out, and I didn't want anyone to see me. There were some flats leaning against the wall in the wings there, and I just crawled behind them and cried!"

"Could you see anything?"

"I didn't look out!" the girl told them honestly. "I was an awful sick cat just then. I just wanted to hide." And Mat drew her close against his side, and she lay there relaxed and comforted.

Inspector Tope asked one other question: "Hews, how could a man go into Miss Cyr's dressing room and not be seen?"

Mat said readily: "Why, no trouble about that. You see, sir, there were windows in the second act set, and a back drop behind them, with buildings painted on it, so that the audience looked across the street, or seemed to. That drop stretched clear across the back of the stage. It wasn't more than three feet out from the door of Lola's dressing room;

you had to be careful not to touch it, crossing back stage while the act was on, because of course if you did it would make the buildings painted on it shiver and shake, make the audience laugh."

"So the door wasn't in sight, unless you were behind that back drop?" Tope insisted. "How about from the flies?"

Mat shook his head. "There wouldn't be anyone up there, probably." And he added: "You could see her door from outside Mr. Hammond's dressing room, of course, or from the wings on the other side, if you were far enough back from the stage."

"People did cross back there, during the act?"

"Oh, yes," Mat assented. "You remember, just before the machine gun business, four of us go into the elevator. Well, the other three don't come on again. Kay drags me on. I'm supposed to be badly hurt. But the other three go around behind the back drop to get to their rooms."

"I went across that way," Clara interjected.

"These three men," Tope urged. "They'd be crossing through there about the time the shooting was going on?"

Mat shook his head. "No, sir," he confessed. "You know, that scene gets the audience plenty. We had little peep holes where we could watch the people out front have a fit while we were supposed to be getting shot!"

"You did that, the night Canter was killed?"

"I guess so," Mat assured him. "You couldn't see much; but we always got a kick out of it. Like reading your own obituary or something."

"Anyone else on that side of the stage?"

"There was a prop man, usually. And maybe a couple of stage hands. But you don't notice anything back stage, unless it's something unusual."

Miss Moss seized on this: "You wouldn't notice a man moving about, if you were used to seeing him there?"

"Why, not especially," Mat agreed.

And they were able to learn nothing more; so they turned at last to this more recent tragedy tonight. But in the end Clint began to yawn, and Miss Moss disappeared and came back to whisper to Clara, and then Clara and Mat bade them all good night and departed arm in arm. Clint presently vanished too. It was past three o'clock; that still hour when sleep does rule the world, and silence presses down.

Inspector Tope and Miss Moss sat for a longer while, talking in low tones; but they too were in a sort of waking slumber. These murders ceased to seem of any great import, and by and by they both fell silent, and then he saw her eyes close. He said gently at last that she had best go to her room; and she smiled and assented. She brought a blanket, in case he wished to sleep; she ordered the cushions on the broad couch; she urged:

"And you should lie down! There's no need to worry about me!"

He said with a chuckle: "Nothing much I could do, anyway, ma'am. I don't carry a gun; not much of a hand in a rough-and-tumble any more. But I'll stay around. I might leave, come morning, before you're up; but you'll be all right then."

She said quickly: "I will want to see you tomorrow!"

"I'll come back," he promised; and he cleared his throat and took his courage in his hands. "Even if it weren't for this, I'd come to see you. If you'd let me." He added: "I—want to know you, ma'am."

She smiled, confessing: "I feel as if we'd already known each other a long time, Inspector."

"I'm glad you feel that way," he told her.

And they stood for a little, looking at one another uncertainly, as though each waited for the other to speak. But he could find no word; and she said at last, very gently:

"Is it good night, then?"

"Why, yes, ma'am, good night," he echoed, in something like relief.

And her eyes were dancing as she turned away.

When she was gone, Inspector Tope turned off all the lights save one shaded bulb upon the table, and he lay down and drew the blanket over him. He thought he would not sleep; yet suddenly he did, and woke to find his thoughts full of fragments—disjointed phrases, vague possibilities, doubtful conjectures—out of which abruptly some order seemed to him to appear. If one moved about back stage whose presence there was a customary thing, none might mark what he did or where he went. . . . A watch might be wrong. . . . The door of Lola's dressing room was most easily visible, and most readily accessible, from Hammond's dressing room. . . . A man might pass from one room to the other, behind the back drop without being seen. . . . And—a watch might be wrong. Particularly, wrist watches might be wrong. . . . They were not in general so accurate as other pieces. A watch might be wrong!

He sat up briskly, as though it were important to stick a pin in this possibility before it should escape. He sat up, and he saw gray dawn at the windows peering in. He sat up, and he stood up; and he folded the blanket neatly, and restored the cushions to their places, and found his hat and coat. He went out without a sound, and rang for the elevator and descended through the sleeping building.

There was a policeman in the lobby; the man O'Malley who had been at the theatre the night before. Tope spoke to him. "O'Malley, go upstairs! Stay in the corridor outside 14-A," he directed. "Don't let anyone go in unless you know him."

O'Malley grinned. "Inspector Hagan told me to keep an eye on the girl up there," he assented. "And we've got men in the basement, and the alley behind, to see no one goes out."

Tope nodded. "Good," he agreed. "But you go upstairs, and don't let anyone in, either. That will suit Hagan too."

He saw the other depart to follow his suggestion; and Inspector Tope went on his way. He wished to see Doctor Gero; but in the taxicab it occurred to him that the Medical Examiner had been late abroad, might still be sleeping. So Tope breakfasted, and it was after seven o'clock before he rang the other's bell.

Doctor Gero, roused from sleep, nevertheless did meet him in friendly fashion; they had worked side by side for a long time, these two. Tope came directly to the point.

"I don't figure in this business at all, Doctor," he admitted. "No right to any information. But tell me something, will you?"

The other chuckled. "Certainly," he assented. "Anything you want."

And the old man asked precisely: "Hammond was shot twice?"

"Yes, once through the heart, and once in the face. Through the left wrist, and into his face just below the eye. The bullet hit his wrist watch, drove a piece of the stem of it into the wound!"

"Then his wrist must have been pretty close to his face when the bullet hit him."

"Yes. His hand was driven back against his face. The watch cut his cheek!"

"How long had he been dead when you saw him?"

"An hour or so. The watch stopped at twelve-thirty-eight."

"Which bullet would you say hit him first?"

"Why, the face wound, I suppose. After the other, there'd have been no need to shoot him again."

"Gun was wrapped in a blanket, wasn't it? To kill the sound?"

"Yes."

"Find any pieces of blanket in the wound?"

"Some in the wrist, yes," Doctor Gero agreed. "I didn't notice any in the face, or chest!"

Tope tapped his hand on his knee. "Where's that blanket? Have you got it?"

"Yes."

"Let's look at it," said the older man intently.

And Doctor Gero, after a thoughtful moment, led the way into his office. The blanket was packed in paper there; he unwrapped it and they spread it on the floor to examine the marks it bore.

There were four holes which a bullet might have made. Around one was a powder smut; the others showed this in less degree or not at all. Tope turned the blanket over, looked for a similar smudge upon the other side; and he stood up quickly.

"Only one shot went through this blanket, Doctor," he said. "See! It was folded to make four thicknesses, but one bullet made all four holes."

"That's right," the younger man assented. He looked at Tope. "What does that mean?"

And Tope chuckled with a sudden deep triumph. "You

tell Hagan about it," he directed. "Don't say I told you! Just tell him the man that killed Hammond shot him through the heart; then he turned Hammond's watch ahead, half an hour or so, and got a blanket to muffle the noise, and shot him through the wrist and face!"

"Alibi?" Gero exclaimed.

"You tell Hagan!" Tope repeated; and his eyes were shining. "Let him figure it out. Let him get the man. The way to train a fighting dog is to let him win some battles. It will do Hagan good to win."

"You're not taking a hand?" the Medical Examiner inquired.

"Not unless I have to," Tope promised. "Not unless Hagan misses. I want him to put this through, himself!"

"Who did it?" Gero asked. "Where is he? Won't he get away?"

But Tope shook his head. "He's been on the dodge two months, and he's still in town," he said. "He had reason enough to get away before, but he didn't, and he won't run, now. He's got reasons to stay."

"What reasons?"

"Four hundred thousand of them," Tope chuckled. He turned briskly toward the door. "Phone Hagan, tell him," he urged. "Let him put it through!"

He chose to walk back to his room on Boylston Street. He wished to change his clothes before setting forth upon the final business of this day. He came to his room and telephoned Dave Howell; but Howell was not to be located and Tope left word at Headquarters for him to call.

He got into a tub; and while he dressed he whistled cheerfully, and he moved briskly to and fro. He had only begun to dress again when someone knocked on the door. He called discreetly through the panels:

"Who is it?"

And Miss Moss answered.

Inspector Tope looked at himself in dismay. He protested: "You wait five minutes, ma'am, I'm dressing."

He thought there was faint mirth in her tones. "All right," she agreed. "But—hurry, please! This is important; a matter of time, I think."

"Make it one minute, then," he promised. He tossed his discarded garments into the bathroom, closed the door. He drew the cretonne curtains across the alcove to hide his unused bed. He found his slippers and dressing gown. He combed his hair; and within the promised minute, he had opened the door to her. She came quickly in.

"Good morning," she said.

"Morning, ma'am," he returned; and he told her apologetically: "I didn't dress, but I didn't want to keep you waiting."

"You're quite all right," she assured him smilingly. "Listen, Inspector. I woke with a thought."

"Yes?"

"To shoot a man through the wrist; that doesn't happen often. An accident that fixes the time of the shooting so exactly. Does it?"

"I never knew it to happen this way before! Not in over thirty years." His eyes were twinkling with a deep appreciation of her shrewd intelligence.

"I thought at first the watch might have been wrong," she confessed. "But now I don't think so. I believe this was arranged just to deceive us about the time."

"You do?" he echoed, admiringly. "It might be, at that." And he asked: "But what for?"

"So whoever did it could prove he was somewhere else at the time!"

Tope seemed to ponder this. "But if it was Peace, nobody knows where he was," he pointed out. "So he couldn't prove he wasn't there. . . ."

"It must be someone we know; someone whose whereabouts we know."

He looked at her intently. "What would be your notion about that?" he asked.

She started to speak; then she laughed suddenly, and said: "Now, Inspector, you already know all this; know who it is. You're pretending, trying to flatter me. Aren't you? Honest, please?"

And he wagged his head in a slow confusion. "Why, I own up," he admitted. "Yes, I think I know who did it. But you're smart, to figure it out yourself!"

"You mustn't humor me like a child!" she protested; and he said seriously:

"Ma'am, I like to humor you! I do."

She smiled happily. "Why?" she asked, in a challenging tone. But before he could reply, she said quickly: "Besides, I'm not just guessing. I am very sure." She watched him gravely. "After I woke, and thought, I spoke to Miss Cyr, and then I called her maid on the telephone and asked her . . ."

"Asked her what?" he exclaimed intently.

"Asked her whether Mayhew, Mr. Hammond's man, went down cellar to keep her company that night, during the shooting, as he usually did."

Tope watched her, waiting for the word he knew must come; but while he waited the phone rang, and he picked up the receiver.

"Hello?" he said; and a reedy, masculine voice inquired:

"Inspector Tope?"

"Yes. Speaking."

"I want to ask you something, Inspector. Can you speak freely? Are you alone?"

Tope looked sidewise at Miss Moss. "Yes, sir, all alone," he replied. "What did you want to know?"

And the voice said briskly: "This. Can you tell me . . ."

Then silence.

The Inspector moved the hook. The operator asked:

"Number please?"

"I was cut off, operator."

"With what number were you talking?"

"They were calling me."

"Hang up for a moment and they will call you back!"

Inspector Tope hesitated doubtfully; he set down the telephone, and he said to the woman here beside him: "Someone started to ask me something, and then hung up!"

Miss Moss caught his arm. "Someone wanted to find out whether you were at home!" she guessed swiftly. "Wanted to be sure you were alone . . ."

Instantly he turned and caught up the telephone again, called supervisor, gave his name. "Trace that call, quick!" he directed. "Police business!"

These two waited without speaking till the answer came; the Inspector listened, said a brief: "Thank you." And he turned to Miss Moss again.

"The call came from a drug store two blocks from here," he reported.

"He's coming!" she whispered.

And then they heard a light step on the stair!

It was Miss Moss who in this moment was the first to move. She made a sign for silence; she slipped across the room and parted the curtains which hid the Inspector's bed in its niche in the wall. She disappeared; the curtains were still swaying when a knock sounded at the door.

And Inspector Tope, with no least hesitation, walked across the room to open it. A man stood in the dusky hall; a small man, in some faint fashion familiar. The Inspector nodded, bade him in.

The man entered. He was, Inspector Tope saw, rather past middle life; a precise little man, whose clothes were perfection, whose dark mustache was close clipped, whose eyes were keen. He paused just inside the door, his hat in his left hand, and he said:

"You are Inspector Tope?"

"Yes," Tope assured him. He was trying to remember where he had seen this man before. Also he was relieved that the man's back was toward the curtains that hid the bed.

"My name is Mayhew," the man explained; and Tope remembered. The night of Doctor Canter's death he had caught a glimpse of this man, hanging up a pair of trousers in Hammond's dressing room, going calmly about his usual tasks while disorder moved all around.

Yet he only said: "Mayhew, eh? I don't know you, do I?"

The little man smiled. "I was Mr. Hammond's valet," he explained. "He discharged me yesterday, but he told me you wished a valet. I am open for engagements, sir."

Tope wagged his head. "Pshaw!" he protested in a good-humored tone. "If a man says a fool thing, it sure does get around! No, I was just talking to hear myself talk, I'm afraid."

Mayhew frowned regretfully. "That is a disappointment!"

he confessed; and Tope, more attentive than he seemed, sensed the deep excitement in the man. "A severe disappointment!" he repeated. "When my landlady told me that you came to my boarding house last night, so late, I thought surely you had come to offer me a place!"

Tope looked at him with a mild blue eye. He was ready now.

"You came in such haste, so soon as you knew Mr. Hammond was dead," said Mayhew in a silky tone. And suddenly there was a pistol in his hand. It was level upon Inspector Tope.

"I cannot stand disappointment," said Mayhew very gently. "And I do not like talkative, inquisitive old men, Inspector. Forgive my harsh measures; but if you permit . . ."

The weapon moved a fraction of an inch as his muscles tightened; and then behind him someone said:

"Good morning, Mr. Peace!"

The man leaped back and whirled, to see Miss Moss yonder. Tope, with a speed astonishing in one so old and round, was after him. The gun spat venomously; and then Tope's weight bore him down. The gun cracked again, and Inspector Tope wrenched the smaller man's arm, and the gun clattered against the bricks of the hearth. Then a heel struck upward shrewdly, so that Tope gasped, and for an instant did release his hold. Mayhew was free, was at the door, was through. . . .

Tope after him! His dressing gown tangled about his legs. He fell, and scrambled up again. Yet in a moment more, for all his unseemly garb, he would have been down the stairs and out upon the street in hot pursuit; but he looked back. And then he turned back, Mayhew all forgotten now.

For Miss Moss lay on her face across the floor.

10

INSPECTOR TOPE sprang to Miss Moss, and he lifted her in his arms, turned her awkwardly. She lay on her face; he raised her to a sitting posture, supporting her shoulders with his right arm. He was surprised to find how small she was, how slender, how slight her weight; and he was surprised too by her softness. The Inspector had grappled men in his time; he was accustomed to the solid feel of masculine flesh. But by this soft fragility which he felt now, he was curiously moved and pitiful.

Her cheeks were drained white; she had fainted. And he remembered her prescription for Lola Cyr the night before, so he lifted her incontinently across his knees, himself sitting straight-legged on the floor, in such a way that her head was lower than her body. At the same time he sought for any sign of a wound. There was none upon her head or throat that he could see; but he did discover a small rent in the shoulder of her coat; and when he turned the coat back and stripped the sleeve away, he found a moist dark stain upon the fabric there.

He gripped her arm and moved it slightly, to discover whether the bullet had struck the bone; and when he did so, Miss Moss opened her eyes and looked up at him in a still bewilderment. He burned with a fierce embarrassment, like a child caught in the jam pot. He had always a certain sense of the ridiculous; and certainly this posture in which they found themselves was absurd enough. The plump old man sitting straight-legged on the floor; the woman full-length across his knees. He saw that she had opened her eyes, and he stammered something; and she closed her eyes again and whispered a word he could not hear. He said earnestly:

"It's all right, ma'am, he's gone!"

She was silent as though she had fainted again; but he saw that her color did return. She reached for his hand suddenly, and struggled to sit up. He helped her. She sat up on his lap, and rubbed her eyes with her left hand, clinging to his shoulder with her right.

"Got away?" she asked in a hoarse voice.

"It's all right, ma'am," he repeated. "We'll get him!"

"I'm a little—sick," she confessed, and seemed to wilt against his shoulder.

"He shot you! Just a nick in your arm. Not bad at all. There . . ." And Inspector Tope patted her reassuringly with his pudgy hand.

Without lifting her head she opened her eyes, and saw his dressing gown under her cheek. She looked up then, realizing where she was; and she cried:

"Mercy! We can't sit here!"

"Plenty of time to get him," Inspector Tope urged; but she laughed, and tried to scramble to her feet.

"I mean, on your lap! On the floor! It's not decent, Inspector," she protested, in a deep amusement.

"Why, ma'am," he said, with sudden courage, "it seemed all right to me. I kind of liked it. I did." He was up with her, holding her lest even now she totter and fall.

"In a chair, perhaps," she confessed, still smiling. "But not on the floor!"

He understood that she was laughing at him, or with him; he said seriously:

"You let me look at your shoulder, ma'am. Or would I call a doctor in? Maybe better that, I guess."

"I'm all right now," she assured him. "Let me see! It hurts!" she admitted, as she slipped off her coat; surrendering it to him. She opened the throat of her gown; she made him look to see whether the bullet had emerged at the back of her shoulder. It had, they found, no more than ploughed the skin below her shoulder, between arm and side.

"I'd better get a doctor," he insisted.

She was consenting when the telephone rang to startle them again. He lifted the receiver, and Dave Howell spoke to him. Tope listened, answered; and he told Howell briefly what had happened here.

While he did so, Miss Moss moved away; she went into the bathroom, and when he finished, she called to him:

"Have you iodine, some disinfectant?"

"Not a thing, ma'am! Only whiskey!"

"That will do," she agreed. He fetched the bottle, handed it through the door to her. And she asked:

"Is Inspector Howell coming? I thought you said so."

"Yes, right away. And he's getting Hagan. It's just a question of catching Mayhew, now. Peace, that is to say."

"Never mind a doctor. I can fix this myself, I'm sure," she decided. She was in the bathroom, beyond his sight as he stood outside. "Have you some big, soft handkerchiefs?"

He had, and brought them. He heard her make a little whistling sound as the alcohol bit at her wound. Later, she was forced to appeal to him for help in securing the bandage. He had no safety pins, so had to knot the ends; and she felt his trembling confusion, and asked laughingly:

"Why is it a man never has pins handy? They're always useful. Suppose you lose a button, Inspector, unexpectedly?"

He said: "Is that too tight?" She reassured him. "Then I guess it'll hold," he suggested, and backed out of the bathroom with a great relief. When she reappeared to join him, her garments were all in order again. Then Howell and Hagan came pounding up the stairs, and another, Doctor Gero.

Hagan explained: "You said she was hurt!" He looked at Miss Moss. "So I fetched Doc along."

"A very small hurt," Miss Moss assured him. But Tope urged:

"You'd better let the Doctor look at you, ma'am."

So these two disappeared together; and Howell and Tope and Hagan considered what was now to do. Hagan said honestly: "I didn't have a notion, Tope. Never thought of this Mayhew at all. I couldn't see anything in it but the girl, Miss Jervis. I never can see but one thing at a time!"

But Tope confessed: "I wasn't much ahead of you; and I'd been working on it before Canter ever was killed, so I had a start! I thought it must be Peace, but I didn't know where Peace was." He looked toward the bathroom door. "Till she said last night that Hammond's watch might be wrong, I didn't get on the Mayhew track at all."

And he added: "When I did, I'd ought to have got action quick. But I knew he wouldn't run away." And he said soberly: "He came to kill me this morning, you know. He'd found out I went to his boarding house last night. I guess he figured I was hot on his trail. The man's blood-crazy. Miss Moss spoke to him, just before he pulled on me. That's what gave me a break. But he'll shoot, when we come up with him."

"I've got the town covered," Hagan said. "He can't move far without running into someone. His boarding house . . ."

"He won't go back there," Tope pointed out. "Mind you,

this man can fix himself so you don't know him. The chance is he's got another room somewhere else. He's there now, changing himself over, changing his looks around!"

Miss Moss and Doctor Gero returned to them; and Hagan insisted: "We're bound to get him!"

But Howell said hopelessly: "I've been after him for over two months, now."

Doctor Gero spoke to Tope: "You told me this morning that there were four hundred thousand reasons why he wouldn't run away."

And Howell lifted his head in a quick attention; and Tope nodded.

"Yes," he said. "He stole that much from the Jervis Trust two months ago. He hid out long enough to grow a beard, change his looks. We found out where he was; but he ducked, broke the trail again. But if he'd had the money with him, he'd have left town then. It's somewhere—I'm guessing, but this is a good guess—it's somewhere where he can't get it yet. That's where we'll find him."

"Would he hide it where he couldn't get at it easy?" Hagan objected.

Tope hesitated; but Miss Moss suggested: "Something unexpected may have happened to prevent him. Else why did he kill Doctor Canter? And Hammond?"

Hagan looked at Tope to answer; and the older man said reflectively: "Why, ma'am, you know we figured Canter was blackmailing him. Canter was in on this whole scheme from the first. Peace paid him once; but then he paid him some more the year after. That has the look of blackmail, to me, and Peace would get tired of that. And the reason he killed Hammond . . ."

Miss Moss interrupted suddenly. "I know!" she exclaimed. "I'd forgotten, because it didn't seem to matter, but since Mayhew was Peace . . . Mrs. Hammond—that's Lola Cyr—told me this morning that Mayhew made love to her yesterday. He asked her to leave Hammond and run away with him. She told her husband. I expect that was why Hammond and Mayhew quarrelled, at the theatre last night."

Hagan ejaculated: "What a man!"

"He's crazy," Tope commented. "Money-crazy, and woman-crazy, and blood-crazy. Then he killed Hammond to get this woman!"

They were an instant silent, considering this. But Miss Moss objected:

"Why would he take Hammond down cellar to kill him? And if he didn't take him down, how did he know Hammond would be down there? And if he took him down, how did he make Hammond go?" No one answered, and she said in a deep curiosity: "Why should Hammond go down cellar in his pyjamas, at that time of night?"

And Tope, at that, laughed aloud: a swift, mirthful chuckle. "Boys, we're blind!" he told them. "Blind, and deaf and dumb!" He looked toward Miss Moss proudly. "She'll see it in a minute!" he predicted. "When she knows what you know, Hagan; you and Doctor Gero and me. She'll see!"

"What's that?" Hagan asked. "What are you talking about?"

And for answer Tope spoke to Doctor Gero: "Hammond clean, Doctor?"

"No," Gero confessed. "He couldn't be, sprawling on that floor. He was covered with coal dust."

"Was he dirty all over?"

"Why, all down his back, and his hands and arms."

"You mean, his clothes?"

"No. No, his hands, too. There was coal dust ground into them. Under his finger nails?"

Tope swung expectantly to Miss Moss, and they were all silent, watching her. After a moment she smiled, and spoke in some confusion.

"You mean, what do I think?" she asked. And she said: "Why, I should think Mr. Hammond must have been digging with his hands in the pile of coal!"

Tope banged his fist into his palm. "He and Peace quarrelled over the woman!" he cried exultantly. "But Hammond had helped Peace to hide out, ever since he disappeared, and he rated a cut of the money. He asked for his share, and Peace told him it was buried in the coal down cellar! Told him to come downstairs that night for his split."

Hagan ejaculated: "Buried in the coal? You think . . ."

Miss Moss said swiftly: "I remember something! Just

after Mr. Peace disappeared, the Estate had a chance to buy a lot of steam coal cheap, and we filled the bins. Mr. Peace couldn't have foreseen that. But the new coal would bury the money clear out of reach, till the coal was used." She looked toward Inspector Tope. "And Michelsen telephoned that we'll soon need more coal, while you were in the office yesterday, so the bins must be low!"

"Then it's still there!" Tope exclaimed.

"Unless he got it last night after he killed Hammond," Hagan interjected.

"No!" Tope insisted. "He wouldn't take time. He'd be afraid the first shot had been heard. He took a chance on the second shot, for the sake of an alibi; then he got out of there. There's a lot of coal in that bin still. Take some time to dig into it! I say it's still there!"

Hagan turned sharply to the telephone. "We'll see!" he cried.

But Tope caught his arm. "No. He'll come for it!" he insisted. "That's where we'll grab the man!"

And while they listened, in the end assentingly, he told them all his plan. . . .

The basement of the apartment building in which Miss Moss dwelt was divided into two parts by a wide corridor which extended from the alley door to the freight elevator. On one side of this corridor there were, arranged in blocks, a number of boarded compartments for the storage of baggage and unwanted furniture. There was one of these compartments for each tenant; the whole number was impressive; they made a sort of labyrinth of wooden walls, extending not quite to the ceiling of the cellar.

On the other side of the central corridor were concentrated the heating and other service units. Beginning just beside the doorway into the alley there was a storage space, enclosed; then the small room in which Peace, during his service as a janitor, had lodged. Beyond this again there were three coal bins side by side; each one a concrete vault of considerable proportions, with concrete walls and roof and floor. The floor sloped somewhat toward the furnace room, into which each of these vaults opened. There was another, smaller bin, on the street side of the cellar, in which coal for the hot water heaters was stored; and alongside this bin, a laundry and drying room were provided for the weekly use of tenants.

A narrow hall led off the main corridor passing between this laundry and the room Peace once had occupied, and so came to the furnace room itself. The furnace room was of some extent, with heating units, hot water boilers, fuse boxes, electric refrigeration machines and other apparatus arranged in orderly pattern about the outer walls. There were steel tracks set in the concrete floor, on which a small car ran; and this car, loaded with coal at the bins, could be wheeled readily to the furnaces as desired.

On the evening after that morning when Mayhew came to kill Inspector Tope, the janitor who had succeeded Burke filled the hoppers with coal at eight o'clock so that the automatic feeders would keep the fires supported for the night; then he departed. At about the same time, a patrol wagon picked up the two patrolmen who all this day had stood guard in front of the building; and it rounded the block to collect two others, posted at either end of the alley in the rear. It then clanged away toward the police station, and the neighborhood resumed its normal aspect.

In the basement itself, a single bulb burned in the main corridor, halfway from the alley door to the freight elevator. This bulb was cobwebbed and dingy; the light it shed was dim and uncertain. There was no other illumination than this; it served poorly, and in the shadows it was worse than no light at all.

The basement was dim and silent; but there were sounds in this gray silence. Occasionally one of the refrigerating motors whirred for a while; occasionally the automatic feeders on the furnaces did their appointed task; occasionally there was a gurgling of steam in the water tanks or the clicking of a meter in one of the long rows upon the wall. Sometimes faint sounds emerged from the labyrinth of storage cubbyholes, as though mice, or rats, were busy there.

If there had been anyone to listen for sounds in this noisy silence, the time must have seemed to him to drag interminably. From eight o'clock in the evening till half after one at night is in fact a very long time, unless you are sleeping. And even to a sleeper, if he be a man rather old and rather tired, who sleeps uncomfortably with his back propped against a concrete wall and his legs cramped against the rear end of a warm furnace, it may still seem long if he wakes from his slumbers now and then.

Sometimes, when he thus awoke, Inspector Tope began to think he must have been mistaken. Yet for all his doubts, he waited as patiently as he could, comforted by the thought that the others here must be as uncomfortable as he. And at a little after half-past one, he knew his waiting had not been vain; for a faint, cool current of night air came trickling across the floor to touch his legs. There was a window open somewhere, or a door!

Until now, the night had seemed full of silence; but now when one wished to hear, there were so many small sounds to confuse the ears. But by and by the Inspector did distinguish the soft, sibilant whisper of sliding coal; of fine coal sliding down to fill a cavity in the flank of the pile. And later this sound was repeated, and still later it was repeated again.

When presently the old man looked at his wrist watch, careful to keep the luminous dial concealed, he saw that it was more than half an hour since he first felt that trickle of cold night air. Later, it was near an hour!

And then, abruptly and without any warning, the lights came crashing on. The sudden illumination had the effect of cymbals, of a hideous din. It could set a man's heart pounding dreadfully. Inspector Tope was sick with it; there was a moment when he could not move.

But he did move then, to look cautiously around the corner of the furnace which protected him. He peered out, and he saw a man who must be Peace, standing in the middle of the furnace room, with a small leather case, covered with coal dust, on the floor at his feet.

This must be Peace; there was no likelihood that any other would be here. Yet save for his stature there was nothing to suggest his identity. When the lights came crashing on, he was just stepping out of an overall suit of the sort mechanics wear; he stood there clad only in his undergarments, with rubber gloves upon his hands, halfway up his arms. And his face was black with coal, the whites of his eyes gleaming.

Another bag was open at his side, and a suit of clothes lay ready there.

He wore one thing more; a shoulder holster strapped over his underclothes.

And for an instant after the lights came on, the little man stood motionless, shaken by the shock of that sudden illumination. Then his gun was in his hand! He balanced the weapon easily, and his teeth shone in the sooty blackness that was his countenance, and he called in a mocking tone:

"All right, who's first, gentlemen?"

He was pilloried in the light, immolated as though upon a pedestal, fifteen feet from the nearest cover. Blackness ringed him in. There were shadows all about him, in which many men might hide.

"Come, who's first?" he repeated insistently.

Hagan spoke, from inside the laundry door, invisible.

"Drop your gun, Peace," he said.

"Nonsense," the man retorted gaily. "Shoot if you must this old gray head! I'd as soon go now. Or show yourself, if you've got insides in you, and we'll talk it over. Here I am! Who's first, my friends?"

No one answered; and the man asked challengingly: "Where's the old fat one, Inspector Tope? I believe he'd come out if he were here. No fear in that old man! Inspector, are you there?"

"Sorry, Peace," Tope called. "I can't oblige. Better drop your gun. They'll shoot your legs out from under you."

"You won't come?" Peace echoed. "Man, you disappoint me, fair!" He hesitated; and he laughed again. "Why, gentlemen, if you won't oblige," he protested, "I suppose I'll have to leave you. . . ."

Hagan said sternly: "There are two men behind you, Peace. There are two here with me, and two more back of the furnaces, and two down by the light switches, and a dozen more outside. There's no chance for you to get away!"

Peace echoed mockingly: "No escape at all? You are not particularly acute, my friend. May I show you one road you cannot close? Observe!"

And he lifted the muzzle of his weapon, with an almost indolent gesture, to his brow.

And a shot roared and reverberated against the concrete walls.

But it was not his gun which was discharged! A bullet struck the weapon from his hands; the pistol rebounded with a metallic sound across the floor. The man shook his stinging fingers ruefully; he seemed to crouch; he whispered, as though suddenly in pity for himself:

"Eh, but the game's never fair!"

And suddenly like a cat he moved; he was gone!

Tope had predicted that Peace would come by way of the window of that room he formerly had occupied; so the room had been left untenanted to make his entrance easy. That way now he ran. Hagan was after him; but the smaller man moved two feet to Hagan's one.

He might have made clean away. But a door that is left open may be closed after a man has gone in, so that he cannot come out again. It was thus they dealt with Peace now. He scrambled through the window—into waiting arms. . . .

There was, they found, a certain pride in the man. With the abnormal vanity of the essentially criminal mind he talked to them freely; to Tope, and Hagan and Dave Howell, and the other lesser figures who did cluster 'round.

It was at first a sporting proposition, he said. He discovered in himself a gift for mimicry; he amused himself, on three or four occasions, by devising some disguise and confronting his closest friends to their befoolment. Later, he perceived possibilities of profit in this gift, and laid a deeper plan, with Canter and eventually Hammond for his confederates.

Canter was a rogue at heart, he said; Hammond had suffered once through poverty. Cupidity could drive them both to any end. They would serve him so long as they served without risk and were well paid. "So I faked the automobile accident," he boasted. "Canter came along right behind me. I nosed into a tree, and he picked me up—I wasn't hurt at all—and took me into his hospital right next door. And during the next two years I built up the Peace the world knew by sight." He added with a grin: "Canter began to increase the price; but I paid. I could dismiss him when the time came. He and Hammond, too!"

Hagan prompted: "And you did dismiss them?"

"Canter was luck!" the man admitted. "I expected some trouble in arranging that. But he came to see Lola; and—I wanted her myself. Then the little Jervis girl dropped a gun right under my eyes. I had only to pick it up, wait for the proper time, walk from Hammond's dressing room to Lola's, shoot him, shove him out of sight and get back to Hammond's room again."

Howell asked: "How did you get away, the night we lost you, two months ago?"

And the man chuckled. "I didn't. I took on a new job," he explained. "Two of them, in fact. I became Burke, the janitor, in the daytime; I was Mayhew at night. I was already Mayhew when I left the theatre that night. You didn't inquire; but anyone would have told you that Mayhew had been losing weight these two months gone, as fast as Burke did. I talked to you myself one evening. Remember, Inspector Howell?" His eyes were all derisive.

He confirmed Tope's guess in the matter of Hammond's death. Hammond, infuriated by Peace's attempt to persuade Lola to run away with him, had demanded that they divide the loot and separate. Peace told him the bonds were hidden in the cellar.

"I hadn't quite decided to kill him," he explained. "But I found the rat digging in the coal, trying to get the stuff himself. So that was that!"

And when he was done, he answered their questions with the utmost freedom, till at last Hagan said:

"Well, that's all, I guess. We'll move."

So they took him away; but Tope and Dave Howell carried the little leather bag with its rich contents up to show to Miss Moss. She was waiting for them, with the young folk. They had to hear the story; and then Dave Howell departed taking the treasure with him for safe-keeping. and the others talked for long, going over and over every aspect of the tale

Till at last Clint was sleepy, and Mat and Clara likewise went to their room, and Miss Moss and Inspector Tope were left alone.

Silence held them for a space. He said then, doubtfully: "I

don't know as you're pleased, ma'am. Having the bonds back. But it had to be that way."

She smiled faintly. "Why, I'm not worried now," she assured him. "Clara has found herself. I like Mat." She added: "I didn't like Kay as much as Clint did, but that has—cleared up, too."

He considered this, and he looked at his hands where they rested on his plump knees. "If you haven't got them to look out for, you'll be kind of out of a job, ma'am, it seems to me," he said at last, and his throat was dry.

"There's always the Trust," she pointed out. "Although Clint will soon be handling that."

"So you won't have a thing to do at all," he insisted.

"Not a thing!" she agreed, with a gay lift in her tones. "Unless, of course, someone else comes along to—offer me a job!"

He cleared his throat sharply, and he swallowed hard. "Why, ma'am—" he began, and hesitated then; and presently the old Inspector wagged his head and smiled.

"Why, ma'am," he said, "I guess we'd get along a lot faster with this business if you tell me your first name!"

THE END

TO THE READER

If you enjoyed this book, you will be glad to know that there are many others just as well written, just as interesting, to be had in the Fiction House Press Library.

You will find the Fiction House Press Library online at

www.FictionHousePress.com

www.ingramcontent.com/pod-product-compliance
Lightning Source LLC
LaVergne TN
LVHW090954080826
845145LV00003B/1011

* 9 7 8 1 6 4 7 2 0 1 8 5 2 *